D1326940

MAX BLECHER

OCCURRENCE IN THE IMMEDIATE UNREALITY

Translated by Alistair Ian Blyth

Featured Artist
ANCA BOERIU

University of Plymouth Press

20 ROMANIAN WRITERS SERIES

Max Blecher's *Occurrence in the Immediate Unreality* is among the first four titles to be published in the series 20 Romanian Writers by the University of Plymouth Press. The series is one aspect of the University of Plymouth's ongoing commitment to bringing Romania's vibrant artistic culture to the West. In addition to the literature, the University of Plymouth will be hosting a series of exhibitions and performances of Romania's visual and musical arts over the next five years.

The following supplement features one of Romania's leading contemporary artists.

Featured Artist

ANCA BOERIU

Anca Boeriu (born 1957). One of Romania's leading artists and illustrators, she has been devoted to the study of etching techniques exploring new possibilities for the resonance of elaborate imagery inscribed through use the metal plate. As an artist she is influenced by human bodies that are always in a state of bodily tension, so there is a relationship between Blecher's condition and Boeriu's art – Blecher had spinal TB, and remained in bed for the last ten years of his life.

Boeriu is an associate lecturer at the National University of the Arts, Bucharest. Awards include: First prize for installation, Radio France International, Paris, 1991. Litography award, Tulcea, Romania, 1994.

Liz Wells

Point of Balance
Oil on canvas, 2008

Point of Balance
Oil on canvas, 2008

Point of Balance
Oil on canvas, 2008

Flying
Mixed media, 1999

Point of Balance
Oil on canvas, 2008

Adam and Eve
Mixed media, 1999

Couple
Mixed media,1999

Point of Balance
Oil on canvas, 2008

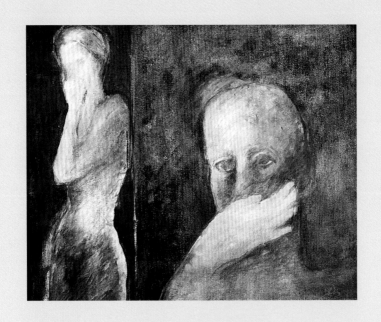

Couple
Mixed media, 1999

Couple
Mixed media, 1999

Couple
Mixed media, 1999

Couple
Mixed media, 1999

Couple
Oil on canvas 2007

MAX BLECHER

OCCURRENCE IN THE IMMEDIATE UNREALITY

Translated by Alistair Ian Blyth

Hardback edition first published in the United Kingdom in 2009 by University of Plymouth Press, Scott Building, Drake Circus, Plymouth, Devon, PL4 8AA, United Kingdom.

ISBN 978-1-84102-207-9

© 2009 Max Blecher
© 2009 Anca Boeriu
© 2009 University of Plymouth Press

The rights of Max Blecher as the author of this work and Anca Boeriu as the artist of this work have been asserted by them in accordance with the Copyright, Designs and Patents Act 1988.

A CIP catalogue record of this book is available from the British Library

Series Editor: Anthony Caleshu
Translation: Alistair Ian Blyth

Publisher: Paul Honeywill
Publishing Assistant: Tanya Sinclair
Series Art Director: Sarah Chapman
Designer: Yulia Razina
Consulting Editor: Liz Wells

All rights reserved. No part of this publication may be reproduced, stored in a retrieval system or transmitted in any form or by any means electronic, mechanical, photocopying, recording, or otherwise, without the prior written permission of UPP. Any person who carries out any unauthorised act in relation to this publication may be liable to criminal prosecution and civil claims for damages.

Typeset by University of Plymouth in Jenson 10/14pt
Printed and bound by R. Booth Limited, Penryn, Cornwall

This book is sold subject to the condition that it shall not, by way of trade or otherwise, be lent, re-sold, hired out, or otherwise circulated without the publisher's prior consent in any form of binding or cover other than that in which it is published and without a similar condition including this condition being imposed on the subsequent purchaser.

Visit www.uppress.co.uk/romanian.htm to learn more about this series

Published with the support of the Romanian Cultural Institute

Contents

Introduction
Alistair Ian Blyth

Max Blecher was born on 8 September 1909 in Botoşani, a provincial town in northern Moldavia, also the birthplace of a number of other important Romanian writers, such as late-Romantic poet Mihai Eminescu, historian Nicolae Iorga, avant-garde poet and artist Isidore Isou (the inventor of "lettrisme"), and, more recently, novelist Dan Lungu. Up until the Second World War, Botoşani was an ethnically and culturally diverse town, whose population was made up of Romanians, Jews, Armenians, Greeks, Roma and Lipovians (Russian Old Believers whose ancestors had fled persecution during the time of Peter the Great). At the turn of the century, Jews made up almost half of the town's population. Max Blecher was the son of a merchant from the town's Jewish community. While he was still a young child, Blecher's family moved to Roman, a Moldavian town south of Botoşani, in the county of Neamţ, where his father opened a porcelain shop. The petty bourgeois Jewish milieu of provincial Moldavia is memorably evoked in his autobiographical *Întîmplări în irealitatea imediată* (*Occurrences in the Immediate Unreality*) (1936), for example in the settings of Eugene's sewing machine shop or the house and office of Blecher's uncle and cousins, the Webers.

After finishing lycée in Roman, Blecher travelled to Paris to study medicine. It was here, in 1928, that he was diagnosed with tuberculosis of the spine, or Pott's disease. He subsequently underwent treatment at sanatoria in France (Berck-sur-Mer), Switzerland (Leysin) and Romania (Tekirghiol), an experience which served as the inspiration for his novel *Inimi cicatrizate* (*Cicatrised Hearts*), in some ways a miniature, more naturalist counterpart to Thomas Mann's *The Magic Mountain*, and which is also described in *Vizuina luminată: Jurnal de sanatoriu* (*The Illumined Burrow: Sanatorium Diary*). However, treatment was of no avail, and Max Blecher was to remain bedridden until the end of his short life. After a decade of illness and suffering, he died, aged 28, on 31 May 1938.

Blecher's literary work dates entirely from the period of his illness. Saşa Pană describes him as having been "paralysed and wracked by pain for ten years, with a few relative intermissions, but his mind voyaged through the most deeply buried mysteries, he burrowed with the tenacity of a miner into the remotest seams of his rich mind, of a body engrafted with abscesses and gangrenes".[1] On 29 June 1930, Blecher made his literary debut with a short prose piece entitled "Herrant", written in Berck-sur-Mer and published in *Bilete de papagal* (*Parrot Papers*).[2] In another short prose piece published in 1934,[3] Blecher describes Berck, home to five thousand patients suffering from tuberculosis of the spine, as a "town of immobility and plaster-casts". Plaster is the material specific to the place, "just as steel is to Creuzot, coal to Liverpool, or petrol to Baku". Similarly, Blecher describes the hallucinatory spectacle of a town whose inhabitants are all paralysed in a recumbent posture and encased in plaster: "Recumbent they go to the cinema, recumbent they take carriage rides, recumbent they frequent places of entertainment, recumbent they attend lectures, recumbent they pay their social visits".[4] Also in 1934, a slim volume of Blecher's poems, entitled *Transparent Body*, was published. In the same year, Blecher published translations from Appolinaire, in *Frize* (*Friezes*) magazine. His own poetry is lyrical and surrealistic, reminiscent perhaps of Paul Eluard, as can be seen in the following strophe, for example: "Your integument/Like a bird in the nest of the heart/In rivers of blood you bathe/And you fly through my fingertips".[5] The following year, in 1935, his parents rented a small house for him in a suburb of his hometown of Roman. Writing on a wooden board propped against his knees, which had remained paralysed in a flexed position, it was here that he finished, during interminable nights of insomnia, the books *Adventures in the Immediate Unreality* (1936), *Cicatrised Hearts* (1937), and *The Illumined Burrow* (posthumously edited and published by Saşa Pană in 1971).

Blecher's literary prose was, to a certain extent, influenced by Surrealism. As an autobiography describing the subject's oneiric, irrational experiences, *Occurrences in the Immediate Unreality* (1936) has been compared with André Breton's *Nadja* (1928), although Saşa Pană was of the opinion that Blecher's novel surpassed and would ultimately outlast that of Surrealism's founder. Blecher himself was fascinated by the controlled, lucid pictorial descriptions of delirium to be found in the work of excommunicated Surrealist outcast Salvador Dalí. In a letter to Saşa Pană, dated 7 July 1934,[6] for example, he speaks of Dalí's "cold, perfectly legible and essential dementia", whose "hyper-aesthetic extravagances of adjusted irrationality" he endeavours to imitate in his own texts: "For me, the ideal in writing would be a transposition of the heightened tension that is released by the paintings of Salvador Dalí". Like Dalí's "paranoiac critical method", Blecher's "surrealism" is therefore not an unmediated, disorganised outpouring of the unconscious, such as that found in the experiments with "automatic writing" made by the doctrinaire Surrealists, but rather a controlled channelling of the irrational life of the mind: "The power of the unconscious is very great. A well-structured unconscious (…) can bring ideas which our conscious mind would never have arrived at. I may thus cite two characteristic manifestations of this power: revelation and inspiration".[7]

It is revelation and inspiration – what James Joyce in his autobiographical fictions of childhood and adolescence (*Stephen Hero* and *A Portrait of the Artist as a Young Man*) refers to as (secular) "epiphanies" – that provide the material for Max Blecher's own Bildungsroman of formative experiences, "occurrences" which take place almost entirely within the confines of the author's own febrile, delirious consciousness. In childhood, Max Blecher suffered "crises" or "attacks" of unreality, in which he experienced rupture both from the outer world of objects, and from the inner world of the self. These crises, narrated in *Occurrences in the Immediate Unreality*, might also be likened to the haunting moments of *Stimmung* evoked by Giorgio de Chirico in his *pittura metafisica*, as well as in his oneiric novel *Hebdomeros* (1929), moments during which inward disquietude is experienced as outward atmosphere, submerging the world in ineffable strangeness and enigma. In psychopathology, this is the eerie atmosphere of heightened but empty significance also experienced by sufferers of dementia praecox during the so-called 'aura' that precedes complete rupture with reality. Psychiatrist and neurologist Klaus Conrad referred to such states of exalted dread as the "Trema", employing a piece of German theatrical slang for stage fright.[8] In this respect it is notable that many of de Chirico's paintings depict the vertiginously tilted boards of theatre stages. Likewise, as we shall see below, Blecher's occurrences in the immediate unreality are also pervaded by a menacing sense of theatricality.

During the state of *Stimmung*, external phenomena are thus imbued with a sense of intense but ineffable significance, which hovers tantalisingly beyond reach. Like de Chirico, who saw the world as a "vast museum of strangeness", Blecher too locates his crises out there in the world; they are intrinsic to various places, "sickly spaces", which thereby become menacing "invisible traps". These crises, which Blecher defines as the "profound sentiment of the world's pointlessness", are thus precisely the anti-epiphany or empty transcendence of Modernism: an anxious, heightened sense of meaningfulness, but one devoid of cognisable content, like the "Anwandlungen eines Fast-Nichts" (fits or attacks of an Almost-Nothing) described by Hugo von Hofmannsthal in *Die Briefe des Zurückgekehrten* (*Letters of Those Who Returned*) (1901). Like the cast of the inner ear whose image obsesses Blecher, people and things are nothing more than the negative image of an immanent emptiness.

Although in time Blecher's crises as such abate, they leave behind them the same "crepuscular state" that used to presage them. As in de Chirico's cluttered paintings of his later metaphysical period, Blecher then discovers in heteroclite, seemingly insignificant objects an "essential nostalgia for the world's pointlessness". Such states, which oscillate between melancholy and exaltation, are also closely intertwined with the ambiguous, confusing, even dream-like, experiences of his sexual awakening as an adolescent. He experiences occurrences as disturbingly artificial and theatrical, while other people are like automatons or mannequins, oblivious that "the certitude in which we live is separated by a very fine pellicle from the world of uncertainties". The world itself becomes an eerie stage set, and many episodes in the novel occur in settings of inherent theatrical artificiality, such as the cinema, a waxworks exhibition, or the prop-cluttered basement beneath the stage of a theatre, where Blecher finds refuge and which thus becomes a symbol of the tiers of conscious and unconscious mind. Blecher himself dreams of being an inanimate waxwork, or else he is haunted by his own photograph, which he chances to see mysteriously displayed in the booth of a travelling fairground photographer and which then takes on a life of its own, threatening to subsume his own existence. In one of the most remarkable episodes in the book, Blecher attempts to escape from the agony of his exacerbated awareness (the "Bewußtseinswelt", as it is called by Gottfried Benn, who similarly yearns to escape the pain of consciousness by regressing to the condition of mindless protoplasm) by descending to the ontological level of amorphous, primal mud.

As a whole, *Occurrence in the Immediate Unreality* teems with unsettling characters and events, refracted through the prism of the author's unique existential "illness". It is a work that deserves recognition as one of the most remarkable texts of European modernism.

Notes

[1] *Cu inimălîngă* M. Blecher, in Max Blecher, *Vizuina luminată*, Bucharest: Cartea românească, 1971, pp. 6-7, quoted in Max Blecher, *Întîmplări în irealitatea imediată. Inimi cicatrizate. Vizuina luminată. Corp transparent. Corespondenţă*, ed. Constantin Popa and Nicolae Ţone, Bucharest: Editura Vinea, 1999, p. 409. Saşa Pană was the pen name of Alexander Binder (1902-1981), a close friend of Max Blecher and an important figure in the Romanian avant-garde. As well as being a writer in his own right, he financed, edited and published unu (one), an avant-garde magazine and, after the War, wrote a number of studies and memoirs about the Romanian avant-garde.

[2] Edited and published by Tudor Arghezi (1880-1967), a major Romanian poet and novelist.

[3] "Berck, oraşul damnaţilor" ("Berck, the Town of the Damned"), Vremea, VII, 358, 7 October 1934; Max Blecher, *Întîmplări în irealitatea imediată. Inimi cicatrizate. Vizuina luminată. Corp transparent. Corespondenţă*, ed. Constantin Popa and Nicolae Ţone, Bucharest: Editura Vinea, 1999, pp. 352-357.

[4] Max Blecher, *Întîmplări în irealitatea imediată. Inimi cicatrizate. Vizuina luminată. Corp transparent. Corespondenţă*, ed. Constantin Popa and Nicolae Ţone, Bucharest: Editura Vinea, 1999, p. 353.

[5] Max Blecher, *Întîmplări în irealitatea imediată. Inimi cicatrizate. Vizuina luminată. Corp transparent. Corespondenţă*, ed. Constantin Popa and Nicolae Ţone, Bucharest: Editura Vinea, 1999, p. 335.

[6] Max Blecher, *Întîmplări în irealitatea imediată. Inimi cicatrizate. Vizuina luminată. Corp transparent. Corespondenţă*, ed. Constantin Popa and Nicolae Ţone, Bucharest: Editura Vinea, 1999, p. 396.

[7] Note from an undated manuscript, quoted by Radu Ţeposu in the Preface to Max Blecher, *Întîmplări în irealitatea imediată. Inimi cicatrizate. Vizuina luminată. Corp transparent. Corespondenţă*, ed. Constantin Popa and Nicolae Ţone, Bucharest: Editura Vinea, 1999, p. 12.

[8] See the chapter 'The Truth-Taking Stare' in Louis A. Sass, *Madness and Modernism: Insanity in the Light of Modern Art, Literature, and Thought* (Cambridge, Mass., 1994), pp. 43-74.

"I pant, I sink, I tremble, I expire"
P. B. Shelley

1

When I gaze for a long time at a fixed point on the wall, what sometimes happens is that I will no longer know who I am or where I am. I sense my lack of identity from afar, as though I had, for an instant, become a complete stranger. With matching strength, this abstract personage and my real person vie to convince me.

In the following instant my identity is regained, like in those stereoscopic views when the two images sometimes separate by accident and only when the projectionist readjusts them, superimposing them, do they all at once provide the illusion of depth. Then it appears to me that my room is of a freshness it did not previously possess. It regains its prior consistency and the objects in it fall back into place, in the same way as in a glass of water a lump of crumbled soil will settle in strata of different, well defined and variously coloured elements. The elements of my room stratify into their own outlines and into the colouring of the old memory I have of them.

The sensation of distance and loneliness in the moments when my everyday self has dissolved into inconsistency differs from any other sensation. When it lasts longer, it becomes a fear, a terror of not being able to regain myself ever again. Afar, an uncertain outline lingers in me, encompassed by a great luminosity, in the same way as objects sometimes loom from the mist.

The terrible question "Who exactly am I?" then dwells in me like an entirely new body, having grown in me with skin and organs that are wholly unfamiliar to me. The answer to it is demanded by a deeper and more essential lucidity than that of the brain. All that is capable of stirring in my body writhes, struggles and rebels more vigorously and more elementarily than in everyday life. Everything begs a solution.

Oftentimes, I regain the room as I know it, as though I were closing and opening my eyes; each time, the room is clearer – just as a landscape looms in a telescope with increasing structure, the more we pierce all the veils of intermediary distances by adjusting the focus.

In the end, I recognise myself and regain my room. It is a sensation of slight intoxication. The room is extraordinarily condensed in its matter, and I am implacably returned to the surface of things: the deeper the wave of uncertainty the higher its crest; never and under no other circumstances does it seem to me more evident than in those moments that each object must occupy the place it occupies and that I must be the one who I am.

My struggle in incertitude then no longer has any name; it is the mere regret that I have not found anything in its depths. What surprises me is merely the fact that a complete lack of significance could have been so profoundly bound to my intrinsic matter. When I have come back to myself and seek to express the sensation, it appears wholly impersonal to me: a mere exaggeration of my identity, having grown like a cancer from its own substance. A jellyfish arm that extended immeasurably and groped among the waves in exasperation before finally retracting beneath the gelatinous sucker. In a few instants of disquietude, I have thus traversed all the certainties and uncertainties of my existence, only to return definitively and painfully to my solitude.

It is then a solitude that is purer and more poignant than previously. The sensation of the world being far off is clearer and more intrinsic: a limpid and delicate melancholy, like a dream we recall in the depths of the night.

It alone still reminds me of something of the mystery and rather sad charm of my childhood "crises".

Except that in this sudden disappearance of identity, I rediscover my descents into the cursed spaces of former times. Only in the moments of immediate lucidity that follow upon the return to the surface does the world appear to me in that unusual atmosphere of pointlessness and desuetude, which formed around me when my hallucinatory trances finally overwhelmed me.

*

It was always the same places on the street, in the house, or in the garden that would provoke my crises. Whenever I used to enter their space, the same faintness and dizziness would overwhelm me. They were invisible traps dotted around the town, in no way distinct from the air that encompassed them. They would ferociously lie in wait for me to fall into the trap of the special atmosphere they contained. If I took so much as a single step and entered such a cursed space, the crisis would inevitably come.

One of those spaces was in the town park, in a small glade at the end of a lane, where no one ever walked. The wild rose bushes and dwarf willows that surrounded it opened on one side onto the desolate vista of a deserted field. There was no place in the world sadder or more abandoned. A dense silence settled on the dusty leaves, in the stagnant heat of summer. Now and then, the echoes of the garrison bugles could be heard. Those protracted, futile calls were achingly sad... Far off, the sun-scorched air quivered vaporously like the transparent steam that hovers over a boiling liquid.

The place was wild and isolated; its loneliness seemed endless. There, I felt the heat of the day was more wearying and the air harder to breathe. The dusty bushes were scorched yellow by the sun, in an atmosphere of consummate solitude. A bizarre sensation of pointlessness floated in that glade, which existed "somewhere in the world", somewhere upon which I myself had happed pointlessly, one ordinary summer afternoon, which in itself had no meaning. An afternoon that strayed chaotically in the heat of the sun, among bushes anchored in space somewhere in the world. Then I would feel more profoundly and more painfully that I had nothing to do in this world, nothing to do except roam through parks – through dusty glades baking in the sun, deserted and wild. It was a roaming which in the end rent my heart.

*

Another cursed place was at the very other end of town, between the high and cavernous banks of the river in which I used to swim with my playmates.

The riverbank had subsided in one place. At the top there was a factory for extracting sunflower seed oil. The husks of the seeds were discarded among the walls of the subsided riverbank. In time the heap grew so high that a slope of dried husks formed, from the top of the bank as far as the water's edge.

It was down this slope that my mates would descend to the water, warily, clutching each other by the arm, their footsteps sinking deeply into the carpet of putrefaction.

The high walls of the riverbank to either side of the slope were precipitous and full of fantastical irregularities. The rain had sculpted fine fissures in long streaks, like arabesques, but as hideous as unhealed lesions. They were lacerations in the flesh of the loam, horrid, gaping wounds.

It was between these walls, which impressed me exceedingly, that I too used to have to descend to the river.

Even from afar and long before reaching the riverbank, my nostrils would be filled with the reek of putrid husks. It readied me for the crisis, like a brief period of incubation; it had an unpleasant and nonetheless delicate smell, as did the crises.

Somewhere within me, my olfactory sense would split in two, and the effluvia of the odour of putrefaction would reach different regions of sensation. The gelatinous smell of the decomposing husks was separated and very distinct from, although concomitant to, their pleasant, warm, domestic aroma of toasted nuts.

As soon as I sensed it, that aroma would, in but a few moments, transform me, permeating all my inner fibres, which it would seemingly dissolve, only to replace them with a more ethereal, indefinite matter. From that moment I would no longer be able to avoid it. A pleasant and dizzying faintness would begin in my chest, hastening my steps towards the riverbank, towards the place of my definitive defeat.

I would descend to the water in mad flight, down the mound of husks. The air would resist me with a density as sharp and hard as a knife's blade. The world's space would tumble chaotically into an immense hole with unimagined powers of attraction.

My mates would gaze frightened at my mad flight. The shingly bank at the bottom was very narrow and at the slightest wrong step I would have been hurled into the river, at a spot where eddies at the surface of the water hinted at great depths.

But I was unaware of what I was doing. Reaching the water, at the same speed, I would skirt the mound of husks and run along the river's edge to a certain spot where there was a hollow in the bank.

At the bottom of the hollow a small grotto had formed, a cool and shady cavern, like a chamber excavated from a rock. I would enter and fall to the ground sweating, exhausted and trembling from head to foot.

When I began to come to my senses, I would discover next to me the intimate and ineffably pleasant décor of a grotto with a spring that spurted sluggishly from the rock and trickled over the ground, forming in the middle of the shingly bank a basin of very limpid water, above which I would bend to gaze, without ever wearying of the wonderful lacework of the green moss at the bottom, the worms clinging to spelks of wood, the slivers of old iron covered in rust and mud, the various animals and things at the bottom of the fantastically beautiful water.

*

Apart from these two cursed places, the rest of the town dissolved into a mush of uniform banality, with buildings that were interchangeable, with exasperatingly immobile trees, with dogs, vacant lots, and dust.

Indoors, however, the crises occurred more readily and more often. As a rule, I could never bear solitude in an unfamiliar room. Should I be made to wait, the delicate and terrible swoon would come within moments. The room itself made ready for it: a warm and welcoming intimacy would seep from the walls, oozing over all the furniture and all the objects. All of a sudden, the room would become sublime and I would feel very happy within its space. But this was nothing more than a deception produced by the crisis; its delicate and gentle perversity. In the following moment of my beatitude, everything would be turned upside down and thrown into confusion. I used to peer wide-eyed at everything that was around me, but the objects would lose their usual meaning: they would be bathed in a new existence.

As if suddenly unpackaged from the thin transparent paper in which they had hitherto been wrapped, their appearance would become ineffably new. They seemed intended for some new, higher, and fantastical use, and in vain did I wrack myself to discover it.

But this was not all: the objects would be seized by a veritable frenzy of freedom. They became independent of one another, but they were of an independence that meant not only their isolation, but also an ecstatic exaltation.

Their enthusiasm to exist in a new aureole would overwhelm me, too: powerful attractions bound me to them, their invisible interconnecting ducts transformed me into an object in the room like the others, in the same way that an organ grafted to raw flesh becomes one with the unfamiliar body by means of subtle exchanges of substance.

Once, during a crisis, the sun shed a tiny cascade of rays onto the wall: a golden, unreal water marbled with luminous ripples. I could also see the corner of a bookcase, with thick leather-bound tomes behind its glass pane, and these real details, which I could perceive from the distances of my swoon, managed to dizzy me and topple me, like a final gasp of chloroform. It was what was ordinary and familiar in objects that disturbed me the most. The habitude of seeing them so many times probably ended up wearing away their external membrane and thereby they appeared to me from time to time as having been flayed down to the flesh: raw, unspeakably raw.

The supreme moment of the crisis would consume itself in a floating outside of any world, pleasant and painful at the same time. Should the sound of footfalls be heard, the room would quickly regain its former appearance. Between the walls there would then take place a dwindling, an extremely small, almost imperceptible diminution of its exaltation; this gave me the conviction that the certitude in which we live is separated from the world of uncertainties by but a fine pellicle.

I would awake in the all too familiar room, perspiring, weary and overcome with a sensation of the pointlessness of the objects that surrounded me. I would notice in them new details, just as it can happen that we discover some unusual detail in an object that has served us daily for years in a row.

The room would preserve a vague memory of the catastrophe, like the smell of gunpowder in a place where there has been an explosion. I would look at the leather-bound books in the cabinet with its panes of glass and in their motionlessness I would detect, I do not know how, a perfidious air of secrecy and complicity. The objects around me never gave up their mysterious attitude, one they ferociously preserved in their stern immobility.

*

Familiar words are invalid at certain depths of the soul. I try to define my crises precisely and all I can find are images. The magic word that might express them ought to borrow something from the essences of other sensibilities in life, distilling from them a new odour in a scholarly composition of perfumes.

In order to exist, it ought to contain something of the stupefaction that overwhelms me when I see a person in reality and then closely follow his gestures in a mirror: then, there is something of the disequilibrium of plummeting in a dream, with the whistle of rushing terror that runs up the spine in an unforgettable instant; or something of the mist and the transparency inhabited by bizarre scenes in glass balls.

*

I envied the people around me, hermetically enclosed in their secrets and isolated from the tyranny of objects. They lived as prisoners beneath raincoats and overcoats, but nothing from without could terrorise or conquer them, nothing penetrated into their wonderful gaols. Between the world and me there was no separation. All that enveloped me permeated me from head to foot, as if my skin were porous. The otherwise highly distracted attention with which I gazed around was not a mere act of will. The world extended its tentacles into me in a natural way; I was riddled with the thousand-fold arms of the hydra. I was forced to ascertain, to the point of exasperation, that I lived in the world I could see. There was nothing to be done against this.

The crises belonged to an equal extent both to me and to the places where they occurred. It is true that some of these places contained a "personal" malevolence of their own, but all the others themselves lay in a trance long before my arrival. And so it was with certain rooms, where I used to feel that my crises crystallised from the melancholy of their immobility and boundless solitude.

Like a kind of equity, however, between the world and me (an equity that plunged me even more irremediably into the uniformity of raw matter) the conviction that objects could be innocuous became equal to the terror that they sometimes inflicted upon me. Their innocuousness came from a universal lack of powers.

I vaguely felt that nothing in this world could last to the very end, and that nothing could be perfected. The ferocity of objects exhausted itself in the world. It was thus that there arose in me the idea of the imperfection of any manifestations in this world, be they even supernatural.

In an interior dialogue which, I think, never came to an end, I sometimes defied the malefic powers around me, just as sometimes I would ignobly adulate them. I practised certain strange rituals, but not without purpose. If, on leaving the house and walking along various roads, I always used to retrace my steps, I did so in order not to describe in my passage a circle in which houses and trees would have remained enclosed. In this respect, my walk would resemble a thread and if, once unravelled, I had not gathered it back up, along the same path, the objects caught in the knot of my steps would have forever remained deeply and irremediably bound to me. If during a rain shower I avoided touching the cobbles in the way of the streams of water I did so in order not to add anything to the action of the water and in order not to intervene in the exercise of its elementary powers.

Fire purifies all. I always used to keep a box of matches in my pocket. When I was very sad, I would light a match and pass my hands through the flame, first one, then the other.

In all these things there was a kind of melancholy at existing and a kind of torment arranged banally within the limits of my life as a child.

In time the crises vanished of themselves, but not without leaving behind their powerful memory in me forever.

When I embarked upon adolescence I no longer had crises, but the crepuscular state that preceded them and the profound sense of the world's pointlessness, which followed upon them, somehow became my natural state.

The pointlessness filled the cavities of the world like a liquid that would have spread in all directions. And the sky above me, the eternally prim, absurd and indefinite sky, took on the colour proper to despair.

In this pointlessness that surrounded me and under that eternally cursed sky I still walk even today.

2

For my crises a physician was consulted, and he uttered an odd word: "paludism"; I was most amazed that my disquietudes, so intrinsic and so secret, could have a name, and a name so bizarre at that. The doctor prescribed me quinine: another subject of wonderment. It was impossible for me to understand how my sickly spaces might be cured, *they* with the quinine *I* was taking. But what disturbed me exceedingly was the physician himself. For a long time after the consultation, he continued to exist and to fidget in my memory with rapid automatic gestures whose inexhaustible mechanism I could not manage to stop.

He was a man small in stature, with an egg-shaped head. The pointed extremity of the egg extended into a black, continually quivering little beard. The small, velvety eyes, his clipped gestures and protruding mouth made him resemble a mouse. From the very first, this impression was so powerful that it seemed only natural to me that, on hearing him speak, he pronounced each "r" sonorously and trillingly, as if while talking he were always nibbling something on the sly.

The quinine he gave me also strengthened my conviction that the physician had something mousy about him. Verification of this conviction came about so queerly and is bound to such important events in my childhood that the occurrence is, I believe, worthy of being narrated separately.

Near our house there was a sewing machine shop where I used to go every day and stay for hours. The proprietor was a young man, Eugene, who had just finished his military service and had found himself an occupation in town by opening this shop. He had a sister a year younger than himself: Clara. They lived together somewhere in an outlying district, and by day they looked after the shop; they had neither acquaintances nor relatives.

The shop was merely a private room, newly let out for trade.

The walls still preserved their living-room paint, with violet garlands of lilac and the rectangular, fading traces of the places where the paintings had been hung. In the middle of the ceiling remained a bronze lamp with a dark-red majolica calotte, its edges covered with green acanthus leaves in faience relief. It was a highly ornamented object, old and outmoded, but imposing, something resembling a funerary monument or a veteran general wearing his old uniform on parade.

The sewing machines were lined up in three orderly rows, leaving between them two wide lanes as far as the back. Eugene took care to sprinkle the floor every morning, using an old tin can with a hole in the bottom. The thread of water that trickled out was very fine and Eugene dextrously manipulated it, tracing erudite spirals and figures-of-eight on the floor. Sometimes he would sign his name and write the day's date. The painted walls evidently demanded such delicacies.

At the back of the shop, a screen of planks separated a kind of cabin from the rest of the room. A green curtain covered the entrance. It was there that Eugene and Clara always used to sit. They ate their lunch there, so as not to leave the shop during the day. They called it "the artistes' cabin" and one day I heard Eugene saying: "It's a genuine 'artiste's cabin'. When I go into the shop and speak for half an hour to sell a sewing machine, am I not acting out a comedy?"

And he added in a more learned tone: "Life, in general, is pure theatre".

Behind the curtain, Eugene would play the violin. He kept the notes on the table and stood hunched over them, patiently deciphering the jumbled staves as though he were untangling a knotted clew of threads in order to extract from them one single fine strand, the strand of the musical piece. All afternoon, a small petroleum lamp used to burn on a chest, filling the room with a dead light and scattering the enormous shadow of the violinist over the wall.

I went there so often that in time I became a kind of additional piece of furniture, an extension of the old oil-cloth couch on which I sat immobile, a thing with which no one concerned himself and which hampered no one.

At the back of the cabin, Clara used to do her toilette in the afternoon. She kept her dresses in a cupboard, and she would peer into a broken mirror propped against the lamp on the chest. The mirror was so old that the silvering had rubbed away in places and through the transparent spots loomed the real objects behind the mirror, blending with the reflected images as though in a photograph with superimposed negatives.

Sometimes she would undress almost completely and rub her armpits with cologne, raising her arms without embarrassment, or her breasts, thrusting her hand between body and chemise. The chemise was short, and when she bent over I could see in their entirety her very beautiful legs, squeezed by well-smoothed stockings. She wholly resembled the half-naked woman I had once seen on a pornographic postcard that a pretzel vendor had shown me in the park.

She aroused in me the same hazy swoon as that obscene image, a kind of void that swelled in my chest at the same time as a terrifying sexual hunger clenched my pubis like a claw.

In the cabin, I always sat in the same place on the couch behind Eugene, and waited for Clara to finish her toilette. Then she would leave the shop, passing between her brother and me through a gap so narrow that she would have to rub her thighs against my knees.

Every day, I would wait for that moment with the same impatience and the same torment. It was dependent upon a host of petty circumstances, which I would weigh up and lie in wait for, with an exasperated and extraordinarily sharpened sensibility. It would be enough for Eugene to be thirsty, for him not to feel like playing, or for a customer to come into the shop to make him abandon the place by the table and then there would be enough free space for Clara to be able to pass at a distance from me.

When I used to go there in the afternoon, as I neared the door of the shop I would extrude long quivering antennae, which would explore the air to pick up the sound of the violin. If I heard Eugene playing, a great calm would come over me. I would enter as softly as possible and say my name aloud on the very threshold, so that he would not think it was a customer and interrupt his playing even for an instant. In that instant, it would have been possible for the inertia and the mirage of the melody abruptly to cease and for Eugene to lay aside his violin and play no more that afternoon. For all that, the possibility of unfavourable occurrences did not cease. There were so many things happening in the cabin… During all the time that Clara was doing her toilette, I would listen for the tiniest sounds and follow the tiniest movements in fear that from them the afternoon might develop into a disaster. It was possible, for example, for Eugene to cough lightly, to swallow a little saliva and suddenly say that he was thirsty or going to the confectioners to buy a cake. From infinitesimally small events, such as that cough, a lost afternoon would emerge monstrous, enormous. The entire day would then lose its importance and in bed at night, instead of thinking at leisure (and lingering for a few minutes on each detail in order to "see" and remember it the better) about the moment when my knees touched Clara's stockings – let me carve, sculpt, caress this thought – I would toss feverishly between the sheets, unable to sleep and impatiently waiting for the next day.

One day, something wholly unusual happened. The occurrence commenced with the allure of a disaster and culminated with an unhoped-for surprise, but in such a sudden way and with a gesture so petty that my entire subsequent joy at it was like a stack of heteroclite objects that a conjurer holds in equilibrium at a single point.

Clara, with a single step, changed the content of my visits in its entirety, giving them a different meaning and new frissons, the same as in that chemistry experiment in which I saw how a single piece of crystal immersed in a test-tube of red liquid instantaneously transformed it into an astonishing green.

I was on the couch, in the same place, waiting with the same impatience as ever, when the door opened and someone entered the shop. Eugene immediately left the cabin. All seemed lost. Clara, indifferent, continued to do her toilette, while the conversation in the shop went on endlessly. Nonetheless, it was still possible for Eugene to return before his sister finished dressing.

I painfully followed the thread of the two events, Clara's toilette and the conversation in the shop, thinking that they might unwind parallel to one another until Clara left the shop, or on the contrary they might meet at the fixed point of the cabin, as in those cinematographic films where two locomotives hurtle towards each other and either meet or pass alongside depending on whether a mysterious hand shifts the points at the last moment. In those moments of waiting I categorically felt that the conversation was taking its course and, on a parallel path, Clara was continuing to apply her powder...

I tried to rectify the inevitable by stretching my knees further towards the table. In order to encounter Clara's legs, I would have had to sit right on the edge of the couch, in a posture if not bizarre then at least comical.

It seemed that through the mirror Clara was looking at me and smiling.

She soon finished rounding off the contour of her lips with carmine and powdering her cheek with the puff one last time. The perfume that diffused through the cabin had dizzied me with lust and desperation. At the moment when she passed by me, the thing I was least expecting occurred: she rubbed her thighs against my knees the same as every other day (or perhaps harder? but this was an illusion of course) with the indifferent air that nothing was going on between us.

There is a complicity of vice deeper and quicker than any verbal understanding. It instantaneously pierces the body like an inner melody and entirely transforms thoughts, flesh and blood.

In that fraction of a second, when Clara's legs touched mine, immense new expectations and new hopes had come to birth in me.

*

With Clara, I understood everything from the very first day, from the very first moment; it was my first complete and normal sexual adventure. An adventure full of torments and expectations, full of disquietudes and gnashing of teeth, something that would have resembled love had it not been a mere continuation of aching impatience. To the same extent that I was impulsive and daring, Clara was calm and capricious; she had a violent way of arousing me and a bitchy joy in seeing me suffer – a joy that always preceded the sexual act and formed part of it.

The first time when the thing for which I had been waiting so long happened between us, her provocation was of such an elementary (and almost brutal) simplicity that that meagre phrase she then uttered and that anonymous verb she employed still preserve in me even today something of their former virulence. It is enough for me to think about them a while longer in order for my present indifference to be bitten away as though by an acid and for the phrase to become as violent as it was then.

*

Eugene had gone into town. We were both sitting silently in the shop. Clara in her afternoon dress, cross-legged behind the window, was absorbed in her knitting. A few weeks had passed since the occurrence in the cabin and between us a severe coldness had suddenly arisen, a secret tension that translated as extreme indifference on her part. We would sit in front of each other for whole hours without uttering a word, but nonetheless in that silence there floated a perfectly secret understanding like the threat of an explosion. I lacked merely the mysterious word that would puncture the membrane of conventionality; I would make dozens of plans each evening but the next day they would strike up against the most elementary obstacles: the knitting that could not be interrupted, the lack of a more favourable light, the silence in the shop, or the three rows of sewing machines, too neatly lined up to allow any significant exchange in the shop, be it even one of a sentimental order.

All the while I would be clenching my jaws; it was a terrible silence, a silence that in me had the definiteness and the outline of a scream.

It was Clara who interrupted it. She spoke almost in a whisper, without raising her eyes from her knitting: "If you'd come earlier today, we could have *done it*. Eugene went into town straight after lunch".

Up until then, not even the shadow of a sexual allusion had filtered into our silence, and lo and behold now, from these few words, a new reality gushes up between us, as miraculous and extraordinary as though a marble statue had risen in the midst of the sewing machines, sprouting from the floor.

In an instant I was beside Clara, I clasped her hand and violently caressed it. I kissed her hand. She snatched it away. "Hey, leave me be", she said, annoyed. "Please come, Clara…" "It's too late now, Eugene is coming back, leave me be, leave me be". I was feverishly touching her shoulders, her breasts, her legs. "Leave me be", protested Clara. "Come now, we still have time", I implored. "Where?" "Into the cabin… come on… it's good there".

And when I said "good" my chest swelled with a warm hope. I kissed her hand once more and forcibly tugged her off the chair. She reluctantly allowed herself to be led, dragging her feet across the floor.

From that day on, the afternoons changed their "customs": it was still a case of Eugene, still a case of Clara and of those same sonatas, but now the playing of the violin became intolerable to me and my impatience lay in wait for the moment when Eugene would have to leave. In the same cabin, my disquietudes became different, as though I was playing a new game on a board with lines traced for an already familiar game.

When Eugene left, the true wait would begin. It was a harder, more intolerable wait than hitherto; the silence of the shop would turn into a block of ice.

Clara would seat herself at the window and knit: every day this was the "beginning", and without a beginning our adventure could not take place. Sometimes, Eugene would go out leaving Clara almost undressed in the cabin: I thought that this might hasten events, but I was wrong. Clara would accept no other beginning than that in the shop. I would have to wait pointlessly for her to dress and go into the shop in order to open the book of the afternoon at the first page, behind the window.

I would sit on a stool in front of her and begin to talk to her, to beg her, to implore her for a long time. I knew it was useless; Clara would accept only rarely and even then she would make use of a ruse, in order not to grant me perfect liberty:

"I'm going into the cabin to take a powder, I have a terrible headache, please don't come after me".

I would swear not to and then follow in an instant. In the cabin, a veritable battle would begin, in which, obviously, Clara's forces were inclined to surrender. Then she would tumble all in one piece onto the couch, as though she had tripped up. She would put her hands under her head and close her eyes as though she were asleep. It was impossible to budge her from that position so much as an inch; just as she was, lying on her side, I would have to tear the dress from under her thighs and press myself to her. Clara put up no resistance to my gestures, but nor did she give me any assistance. She was as inert and as indifferent as a block of wood, and only her intimate and secret warmth revealed to me that she was mindful, that she "knew".

*

It was during this period that the physician who prescribed me quinine was consulted. Confirmation of my impression that there was something mousy about him came in the cabin, and, as I have said, in a manner wholly absurd and surprising.

One day, as I was sitting pressed up against Clara and tearing off her dress with feverish hands, I felt something odd moving in the cabin and – more with the obscure but finely honed instinct of the extreme pleasure I was nearing, which admitted no alien presence, than with my real senses – I guessed that a living creature was watching us.

Frightened, I turned my head and on the chest, behind the box of powder, I glimpsed a mouse. It stopped right by the mirror at the edge of the chest and fixed me with its beady black eyes, in which the light of the lamp placed two gleaming golden pips, which pierced me deeply. For a few seconds, it looked into my eyes with such acuity that I felt the gaze of those two glassy points boring into the depths of my brain. It seemed as though it were meditating on a harsh rebuke to me or merely a reproach. But all of a sudden the fascination was shattered and the mouse fled, vanishing behind the chest. I was certain that the doctor had come to spy on me.

The same evening, when I took the quinine, my supposition was bolstered by a perfectly illogical albeit, for me, valid reasoning: the quinine was bitter; on the other hand, in the cabin the doctor had seen the pleasure Clara suddenly offered me; in consequence, and for the establishment of a just balance, he had prescribed me the most unpleasant medicament that could exist. I could hear him nibbling the judgement in his mind: "The grrreater the pleasurrre, the morrre bitterrr the pill!"

A few months after the consultation, the doctor was found dead on the floor of his house; he had fired a bullet into his brow.

My first question on hearing the sinister news was:

"Were there mice on that floor?"

I needed that certainty.

For the doctor truly to be dead, a pack of mice would necessarily have had to swarm over the body, to bore into it and extract the mousy matter lent to the physician during his life in order to exercise their illegitimate "human" existence.

3

I must have been twelve years old when I met Clara. However far back I rummage through my memories, in the depths of childhood I find them connected to sexual knowledge. She appears to me as nostalgic and pure as the adventure of night, of fear, of first friends. She is in no way distinct from other melancholies and other times of waiting, for example the tedious waiting to become an "adult", which I could physically gauge whenever I shook hands with an older person, trying to delimit the difference of weight and size in my small hand, lost between the knobbly fingers, in the enormous palm of the one who was gripping it.

At no time in my childhood did I ignore the difference between men and women. Perhaps there was a time when for me all living beings were jumbled up in a single limpidity of movement and inertia; I have no exact recollection of this. The sexual secret was always apparent. It was a matter of a "secret" in the same way as it might have been a matter of an object: a table or a chair.

When I examine my most distant memories more carefully, however, their lack of actuality is revealed to me in my fallacious understanding of the sexual act. I used to imagine the female organs in erroneous forms and the act in itself as much more grandiose and strange than as I knew it with Clara. In all these interpretations, however – fallacious, and then increasingly just – there ineffably floated an air of mystery and bitterness, which slowly acquired consistency like a painting by an artist who has set out from amorphous sketches.

*

I see myself as I was when very little, in a nightshirt down to my heels, crying desperately on the threshold of a door, in a yard filled with sunlight, whose gate opens onto a deserted market, a market in the afternoon, warm and sad, with dogs sleeping on their bellies and people lying in the shade of the vegetable stalls.

In the air there is an acrid scent of rotting vegetables, a few large violet flies are buzzing loudly around me, imbibing the teardrops that have fallen onto my arms and making frenetic swoops in the dense and broiling light of the yard. I stand up and carefully urinate in the dust. The earth greedily sucks up the liquid and in that spot there remains a dark patch, as if the urine of an object that does not exist. I wipe my face with my nightshirt and lick away the tears at the corners of my lips, savouring their salty taste. I sit down once more on the threshold and feel very unhappy. I have been beaten.

Just now my father smacked my bare buttocks. I do not very well know why. I am thinking. I was lying in bed next to a little girl the same age as me; we were put there to sleep, while our parents went out for a walk. I did not sense them when they returned and I do not know exactly what it was I was doing to the little girl under the quilt. All I know is that in the moment when my father suddenly lifted the sheet, the little girl had begun to yield. My father turned crimson, he was enraged, and he beat me. That is all.

And so I am sitting on the threshold, I have wept and I have dried my eyes, I am drawing circles and lines in the dust with my finger, I shift my position more toward the shade, I am sitting cross-legged on a stone and I am feeling better. A girl has come to fetch water in the yard and she is turning the rusty wheel of the pump. I listen carefully to the creaking of the old iron, I watch how the water, like the haughty, swishing tail of a silver horse, gushes into the pail, I look at the girl's large, dirty legs, I yawn because I have not slept at all and from time to time I try to catch a fly. It is the simple life that recommences after tears. Into the yard the sun forever pours its overwhelming, torrid heat. It is my first sexual adventure and my oldest memory of childhood.

Henceforward obscure instincts will burgeon, wax, distort and settle within their natural bounds. What should have been both an amplified and ever growing fascination was for me a string of renunciations and cruel reductions to banality; the evolution from childhood to adolescence meant a continuous diminution of the world and, as things started to structure themselves around me, their ineffable look disappeared, just like a gleaming surface clouding over with condensation.

Ecstatic, miraculous, the figure of Walter even today preserves its fascinating light.

When I met him, he was sitting in the shade of a locust tree, on a log, reading a Buffalo Bill comic. The clear light of morning filtered through the thick green leaves in a rustle of very cool shadows. His attire was not at all ordinary: he was wearing a cherry-coloured tunic with buttons carved from bone, deerskin trousers, and, on his bare feet, sandals plaited from straps of white leather. Sometimes, when I want to relive for an instant the extraordinary sensation of that encounter, I gaze for a long time at a Buffalo Bill comic. Nevertheless, the real presence of Walter, of his red tunic in the greenish air under the shade of the locust tree, was something else.

His first gesture was a kind of elastic leap onto his feet, like that of an animal. We made friends instantly. We spoke little and all of a sudden he made a stupefying proposal: to eat locust tree flowers. It was the first time I had met someone who ate flowers. In a few moments Walter was up in the tree gathering an enormous bunch. Then he climbed down and showed me how you ought delicately to detach the flower from the corolla in order to suck only its tip. I tried it for myself; the flower gave a little pop between my teeth, a very pleasant little clack, and in my mouth dispersed a delicate and cooling perfume such as I had never tasted before.

For a short while we remained silent, eating the locust tree flowers. All of a sudden he grasped me tightly by the arm: "Would you like to see our gang's headquarters?"

In Walter's eyes sparks had kindled. I hesitated for a second. "Yes, I would", I answered with a voice that was no longer mine and with an impulse for danger which suddenly erupted in me and which I very well sensed did not belong to me.

Walter took me by the hand and through the little gate at the bottom of the yard he led me to a vacant lot. The grass and the weeds had sprung up there unchecked. The nettles stung my legs as I passed and with my hand I had to move aside the thick stems of hemlock and burdock. At the bottom of the vacant lot we came to a tumbledown wall. In front of the wall there was a ditch and a deep hole. Walter jumped inside and called me to follow; the hole led through the wall and thence we entered an abandoned cellar.

The steps were broken and overgrown with grass, the walls oozed dampness, and the darkness before us was consummate. Walter squeezed my hand tightly and pulled me after him. We slowly descended some ten steps. There we came to a stop.

"We have to stop here", he told me, "we can't go any further. At the back there are some iron men with iron hands and iron heads, growing from the ground. They stand there motionless and if they catch us in the dark they'll throttle us".

I turned my head and gazed desperately at the open mouth of the cellar above, whose light came from a simple and clear world where there were no iron men and where at a great distance plants, people and houses could be seen.

Walter produced a plank from somewhere and we sat down upon it. For a few minutes we were silent once more. It was good and cool in the cellar; the air had a heavy odour of dampness and I would have sat there for hours, isolated, far from the hot streets, far from the sad and tedious town. I felt good enclosed between cold walls, beneath the earth seething in the sun. The pointless hum of the afternoon came like a distant echo through the open mouth of the cellar.

"This is where we bring the girls we capture", said Walter.

I vaguely understood what he must have been talking about. The cellar took on an unsuspected attraction.

"And what do you do with them?"

Walter laughed.

"Don't you know? We do what all men do to women, we lie down with them and… with the feather…"

"With the feather? What kind of feather? What do you do to the girls?"

Walter laughed once more.

"How old are you? Don't you know what men do to women? Don't you have a feather? Look at mine".

He took from the pocket of his tunic a small, black, bird's feather.

In that moment I felt that I was being overwhelmed by one of my usual crises. Perhaps Walter would not have taken the feather out of his pocket had I continued to bear that cellar's air of complete desolation to the very end. In an instant, however, the isolation took on a painful and profound meaning. I now realised how far the cellar was from the town and its dusty streets. It was as if I had grown distant from myself, in the solitude of the subterranean depths beneath an ordinary summer's day. The black, glossy feather Walter showed me meant that nothing else existed in my familiar world. Everything entered a fainting fit where it gleamed strangely, in the middle of a strange room with damp grasses, in the darkness that inhaled the light like a cold, ravenous mouth.

"What's up with you?" Walter asked. "Let me tell you what we do with the feather…"

The sky outside, through the mouth of the cellar, became whiter and whiter, more vaporous. The words tapped up against the walls, they softly slid down me like some fluid creature.

Walter went on talking to me. But it was as if he was so far away from me and so ethereal that he seemed a mere clear space in the dark, a patch of mist palpitating in the shadow.

"First you stroke the girl", I heard him as though in a dream, "then, also with the feather, you stroke yourself… These are the things you have to know…"

All of a sudden Walter drew closer to me and began to shake me, as though to wake me from sleep. Slowly, slowly, I began to come round. When I had fully opened my eyes, Walter was bending over my pubis, with his mouth tightly stuck to my sex. It was impossible for me to understand what was going on.

Walter stood up.

"See, that made you better… In the war, the Indians wake their wounded like that and in our gang we know all the Indian spells and cures".

I awoke groggy and exhausted. Walter ran off and vanished. I too climbed the steps, cautiously.

In the days that followed, I sought him everywhere, but in vain. It had been agreed that I should meet him in the cellar, but when I went there it seemed wholly altered. Everywhere there were heaps of garbage, with dead animals and putrefaction that reeked dreadfully in the sun. With Walter I had not seen anything of this. I gave up going to the cellar and thus I never met Walter again.

*

I procured a feather, which I kept in great secrecy, wrapped up in a piece of newspaper in my pocket. It sometimes seemed to me that I myself had invented the whole story with the feather and that Walter had never existed. From time to time I would unwrap the feather from its newspaper and gaze at it for a long while: its mystery was impenetrable. I would brush its silky soft gloss across my cheek and that caress would cause me to shudder a little, as though an invisible, albeit real, person were touching my face with his fingertips. The first time I made use of it was one beautiful evening, in circumstances that are quite extraordinary.

I liked to stay outside until late. That evening a heavy and oppressive storm had sprung up. All the heat of the day had condensed into an overpowering atmosphere, under a black sky slashed by streaks of lightning. I was sitting on the threshold of a house and watching the play of the electric light on the walls of the lane. The wind was shaking the light bulb that illuminated the street, and the concentric circles of the globe, casting shadows onto the walls, were rocking like water sloshing in a pot. Long streamers of dust were being whipped up in the road and rising in spirals.

All of a sudden within a shroud of wind it seemed to me that a white marble statue was rising into the air. There was in that moment a certitude that was unverifiable, like any other certitude. The white block of stone was rapidly receding into the air, in an oblique direction, like a balloon released from a child's hand. In a few moments the statue became a mere white patch in the sky, as big as my fist. Now I could distinctly see two white figures, holding hands and gliding across the sky like skiers.

In that moment a little girl came to a stop in front of me. I must have been sitting open-mouthed and gazing wide-eyed aloft because she asked me in astonishment what it was I could see in the sky.

"Look… a flying statue… look quick… soon it will vanish…"

The girl looked carefully, knitting her brows, and told me she could not see anything. She was a girl from the neighbourhood, plump, with ruddy cheeks like medicinal rubber, her hands forever moist. Up until that evening I had spoken to her only rarely. And as she stood there before me she suddenly began to laugh:

"I know why you tricked me…" she said, "I know what you want…"

She started to move away from me, hopping. I stood up and ran after her; I beckoned her into a dark passageway and she came without resistance. Then I lifted up her dress. She allowed herself to be manhandled, docilely holding onto my shoulders. Perhaps she was more surprised at what was happening than aware of the immodesty of the deed.

The most surprising consequence of this occurrence took place a few days later in the middle of a square. A few builders were slaking quicklime in a bin. I was looking at the seething quicklime when all of a sudden I heard my name called out and someone said loudly: "With the feather, you mean to say… with the feather… eh?" It was a lad of about twenty, a ginger and insufferable lout. I think he lived in a house down that passageway. I glimpsed him for no more than a moment, shouting at me, on the other side of the bin, emerging fantastically from the vapours of the quicklime like a hellish apparition, speaking in the midst of fire and cracks of thunder.

Perhaps he said something else to me, and my imagination lent his words a meaning about which I was preoccupied in those days; I could not believe that he had really seen me in the compact darkness of the passageway.

Nonetheless, thinking about this thing more carefully, it occurred to me that the passageway was not as obscure as it had appeared to me and that everything had been visible (perhaps we had even been standing in the light)... all these were as many suppositions which strengthened my conviction that during the sexual act I was possessed by a dream that muddied my sight and my senses. I imposed greater prudence upon myself. Who knows to what aberrations I was capable of abandoning myself, in broad daylight, in the thrall of excitement and possessed by it like a heavy sleep in which I moved unaware?

Closely connected to the memory of the feather a very disturbing little black book also comes to mind. I had found it in a row of books on a table and leafed through it with great interest. It was a banal novel, *Frida* by André Theuriet, in an illustrated edition with a great number of drawings. In each drawing recurred the image of a young boy with curly blond hair, in velvet garb, and a plump little girl, in a flouncy dress. The little boy resembled Walter. The children appeared in the drawings now together, now separately; it was plain to see that they met above all in the nooks of a park and beneath ruined walls. What did they do together? This is what I would have liked to know. Did the young boy have a feather like mine, which he kept in the pocket of his coat? In the drawings this thing was not visible and I had no time to read the book. A few days later, the little black book vanished without trace. I began to seek it everywhere. I asked at bookshops but it seemed that no one had heard of it. It must have been a book full of secrets given that it was not to be procured anywhere at all.

One day I plucked up courage and went into the public library. A tall, pale man with slightly quivering spectacles was sitting at the back of the room and watched me as I approached. I could no longer turn back. I had to advance as far as the table and there pronounce distinctly the sensational word "Fri-da", like a confession, before that myopic man, of all my hidden vices. I approached the lectern and murmured in a hushed voice the name of the book. The librarian's spectacles started to quiver more noticeably on his nose; he closed his eyes as though he were seeking something in his memory, and he told me that he had not heard of it. The quivering of his spectacles nevertheless seemed to me to betray an inner disturbance; I was now sure that *Frida* contained the most secret and most sensational revelations.

Many years later I found the book on the shelves of a bookshop. It was no longer my little book bound in black cloth but a lowly and wretched pamphlet with yellowed covers. For an instant I wanted to purchase it, but I changed my mind and put it back on the shelf. It is thus that I still preserve intact within me the image of a little black book in which lingers a little of the authentic perfume of my childhood.

4

In small and insignificant objects: a black bird's feather, a nondescript little book, an old photograph with fragile and outmoded personages, seemingly afflicted with a serious internal illness, a delicate green faience ashtray, moulded like an oak leaf, forever smelling of stale ash; in the simple and elementary recollection of old man Samuel Weber's spectacles with their thick lenses, in such trifling ornaments and domestic things can be discovered all the melancholy of my childhood and that essential nostalgia for the world's pointlessness, which enveloped me everywhere, like water with petrified ripples. Gross matter – in its deep, heavy masses of earth, rocks, sky or waters – or in its most incomprehensible forms – paper flowers, mirrors, glass marbles with their enigmatic inner spirals, or tinted statuettes – forever suspended in a confinement that struck painfully against its walls and perpetuated in me, without meaning, the bizarre adventure of being human.

Whithersoever my mind might wend, it encountered immobile objects, which were like walls before which I had to fall upon my knees.

Terrorised by their diversity, I used to think of the infinite forms of matter and for nights on end I would writhe, agitated by series of objects that filed endlessly through my memory, like escalators ceaselessly unfolding thousands and thousands of steps.

At times, in order to dam the torrent of things and colours that flooded my brain, I would imagine the evolution of a single outline, of a single object.

For example, I would imagine – and this as a precise inventory of the world – the chain of all the shadows on earth, the strange and fantastical ashen world that slumbers at life's feet.

The shadow man, spread like a veil over the grass, with spindly legs that trickled like water, with arms of darkened iron, walking among the horizontal trees and their flowering branches.

The shadows of vapours gliding upon the sea, shadows as unstable and aquatic as transient sadnesses, skimming over the foam.

The shadows of birds in flight, black birds rising from the depths of the earth, from a sombre aquarium.

And the solitary shadow, lost somewhere in space, of our spherical planet…

At other times I would think of caverns and hollows, from the vertiginous heights of chasms in the mountains to the warm, elastic, ineffable sexual cavern. I had procured from somewhere or other a small electric torch and in bed at night, maddened by insomnia and by the objects that kept filling my room, I would crawl under the quilt and examine with taut attention, in a kind of aimless but painstaking study, the wrinkles of the sheet and the little clefts that formed between them. I needed such a precise and trifling occupation in order to calm myself to some degree. On one occasion my father found me at midnight rummaging under the pillows with the torch and he took it away from me. Nonetheless, he did not make any remarks and nor did he scold me. I think that for him the discovery had been so odd that he could find neither the words nor the morals that would have applied in the case of such an event.

A few years later, I saw in an anatomy book the photograph of a wax cast of the inner ear. All the canals, sinuses and cavities consisted of full matter, forming their positive image. This photograph made an exceeding impression upon me, almost to the point of faintness. In an instant I realised that the world might exist in a reality that was more authentic, as the positive structure of its empty spaces, so that everything that is hollowed out would become full, and actual reliefs would be transformed into voids of identical shape, without any content, like those delicate and bizarre fossils that reproduce in stone the traces of some shell or leaf which over the course of time has been macerated, leaving nothing but the sculpted, fine imprint of its outline.

In such a world people would no longer be multicoloured, fleshy excrescences, full of intricate and putrescible organs, but rather pure voids, floating like bubbles of air through water, through the warm, soft matter of the full universe. It was also the intrinsic and painful sensation that I often felt in adolescence, when throughout endless wanderings, I used suddenly to find myself in the midst of a terrible isolation, as if around me people and their houses had all of a sudden become gummed up in the compact and uniform jelly of a single material, in which I existed merely as a void that meaninglessly moved to and fro.

*

In ensemble, objects formed stage sets. The impression of the theatrical everywhere accompanied me with a feeling that everything was unfolding in the midst of a factitious and sad performance. When I sometimes escaped from the tedious, matte vision of a colourless world, its theatrical aspect would then appear, emphatic and old-fashioned.

Within the framework of this overall theatricality, there were other, more astonishing theatrical performances which drew me more because their artificiality and the actors playing in them seemed genuinely to understand the mystifying meaning of the world. They alone knew that in a stage-set universe of theatrical performance life had to be acted artificially and ornamentally. Such performances were the cinema and the wax museum.

Oh, the auditorium of the B Cinema, long and dim like a submerged submarine! The doors of the entrance were covered with crystal mirrors in which a part of the street was reflected. At the very entrance itself there was thus a free show, even before the one in the auditorium, an astounding screen on which the street flickered in a greenish dream-like light, with people and carriages that moved somnambulistically in its waters.

In the auditorium a reeking and acidic public baths sultriness reigned. The floor was made of cement and when the chairs were moved they made screeching noises like brief and desperate screams. In front of the screen a gallery of louts and idlers cracked sunflower seed husks between their teeth and commented aloud on the film. Dozens of voices simultaneously spelled out the titles syllable by syllable, like literacy classes at a school for adults. Directly below the screen an orchestra played, made up of a woman pianist, a violinist and an old Jew who energetically plucked the contrabass. That old man also had the task of emitting various sounds corresponding to the action on screen. He would cry out "cock-a-doodle-do" when at the beginning of the film there appeared the cockerel of the movie company, and once, I remember, when the life of Jesus was being depicted, at the moment of the resurrection he began frenetically to thump the body of his bass with the bow to imitate the heavenly thunderclaps.

I lived the episodes in the films with an extraordinary intensity, integrating myself into the action as a veritable character in the drama. It happened to me many times that the film would absorb my attention so much that all of a sudden I would imagine that I was walking through the parks on the screen, or that I was leaning against the balustrade of the Italian terraces on which Francisca Bertini was acting, with pathos, her hair untrammelled and her arms fluttering like scarves.

In the end, there is no well-defined difference between our real self and our various imaginary inner characters. When the lights came up in the interval, the auditorium would have an air of returning from afar. It was in a somewhat precarious and artificial atmosphere, much more uncertain and ephemeral than the performance on the screen. I used to close my eyes and wait until the mechanical munching sound of the apparatus announced that the film was about to continue; then I would find the auditorium in darkness once more and all the people around me, illumined indirectly by the screen, pale and transfigured like a gallery of marble statues in a museum lit by the moon at midnight.

On one occasion there was a fire in the cinema. The film reel had snapped and instantly burst into flames. For a few seconds, the flames were projected onto the screen, as if a candid warning that the cinema was burning. At the same time it was a logical extension of the projector's role of presenting "the news". Its mission had thus, in an excess of perfectionism, led it to present the final and most exciting news item of all, that of its own incineration. Screams erupted from every side, and short cries of "Fire! Fire!" rapped out like revolver shots. In an instant so much noise gushed from the auditorium that it seemed the audience, up until then in silence and darkness, had been doing nothing more than cramming itself with screams and uproar, like calm and innocuous accumulators which explode once their charge capacity is violently exceeded.

In a matter of minutes and before half of the auditorium could be evacuated, the "fire" was put out. Nevertheless, the audience continued to scream, as if they had to exhaust a certain quantity of energy once it had been released. A young miss, her cheeks powdered like a plaster cast, was shrieking stridently, looking me straight in the eyes, without making any movement or taking a single step toward the exit. A brawny lout, confident of the usefulness of his strength in such cases, but nonetheless not knowing how exactly to apply it, was picking up the wooden chairs one by one and hurling them at the screen. All of a sudden a loud and very resonant boom was heard; one chair had landed on the old musician's contrabass. The cinema was full of surprises.

*

In summer, we would go into the matinee early and leave in the evening, as night was falling. The light outside would be altered; the remnants of the day had been extinguished. It was thus I ascertained that in my absence there had occurred in the world an event immense and essential, its sad obligation of always having to continue – by means of nightfall, for example – its repetitive, diaphanous and spectacular labour. In this way we would enter once more into the midst of a certitude that in its daily rigorousness seemed to me of an endless melancholy. In such a world, subject to the most theatrical effects and obligated every evening to perform a proper sunset, the people around me appeared like poor creatures to be commiserated for the seriousness with which they always busied themselves, the seriousness with which they believed so naïvely in whatever they did or felt. There was but one creature in the town who understood these things and for whom I held a respectful admiration: it was the town's madwoman. She alone in the midst of rigid people crammed to the very tops of their heads with prejudices and conventions, she alone preserved her liberty to shout and to dance on the street whenever she wished. She went in rags on the street, corroded by grime, gap-toothed, her red hair dishevelled, holding in her arms with maternal tenderness an old coffer full of crusts of bread and various objects picked from the garbage.

She would show her sex to passers-by with a gesture which, had it been used for any other purpose, would have been called "full of elegance and style". "How splendid, how sublime it is to be mad!" I used to say to myself, and I realised with unimaginable regret how many powerful, familiar, stupid habits and what a crushing, rational education separated me from the extreme freedom of a madman's life.

I think that whoever has not had this sensation is condemned never to feel the true breadth of the world.

*

The general and elementary impression of the theatrical turned into authentic terror as soon as I entered the wax museum with its mannequins. It was a fear mixed with a tinge of vague pleasure and somehow with that bizarre feeling we each sometimes have of previously living in a certain setting. I think that if the urge for an aim in life were ever to arise in me and if this impulse had to be bound to something that is indeed profound, essential and irremediable in me, then my body would have to become a mannequin in a wax museum and my life a simple and endless contemplation of the display cases of the dioramas.

In the gloomy light of the carbide lamps I used to feel that I did indeed live my own life in a unique and inimitable way. It was as if all my everyday actions had been shuffled like a deck of cards. I felt no attachment to them; people's irresponsibility towards their most conscious acts was a fact whose obviousness was plain to see. What importance did it have whether it was I or another who committed them, as long as the variousness of the world enveloped them in the same uniform monotony? In the wax museum, and only there, no contradiction existed between what I did and what occurred. The waxwork figures were the only authentic thing in the world; they alone falsified life in an ostentatious way, becoming part of the true atmosphere of the world through their strange and artificial immobility. The bullet-riddled and blood-stained uniform of some Austrian archduke, with his sad, yellow visage, was infinitely more tragic than any real death. In a crystal casket there lay a woman dressed in black lace, with a pale and gleaming face. An astonishingly red rose was fixed between her breasts, and the blonde wig at the edge of her forehead was coming unglued, while in the nostrils the red colour of the make-up flickered and the blue eyes, as clear as glass, gazed on me motionlessly. It was impossible for the waxwork woman not to have a profound and disturbing significance, one known to no one else. The more I contemplated her the more her meaning seemed to become clear, lingering vaguely somewhere inside me like a word that I was trying to recollect and of which I could grasp only its faraway rhythm.

*

I have always had a bizarre attraction for feminine trinkets and for cheaply ornamented artificial objects. A friend of mine used to collect the most various found objects. In a mahogany box he kept hidden a strip of black silk with very fine lace at the edges, to which were sewn a few glinting glass disks. It was, of course, torn from an old ball gown; in places the silk had begun to moulder. To see it I used to give him stamps and even money. Then he would lead me into a salon in the old style, while his parents were sleeping, and show me it. I would remain with the piece of silk in my hand, mute with stupefaction and pleasure. My friend would stand in the doorway and keep a look out in case anyone came; in a few minutes he would return, take the silk from me, put it in the box and say, "Enough, now it's over, you can't have any longer", which was the same thing Clara sometimes used to say to me when the lingering in the cabin lasted too long.

Another object that disturbed me exceedingly when I saw it for the first time was a gypsy ring. I think it was the most fantastical ring ever to have been invented by man to adorn the hand of a woman.

The extraordinary masked-ball ornaments employed by birds, animals and flowers, designed to play a sexual role; the stylised and ultra-modern tail of a bird of paradise; the rust-coloured feathers of the peacock; the hysterical lacework of petunia petals; the wholly unlifelike blue of a monkey's chops – these are but feeble attempts at sexual ornamentation compared with the dizzying gypsy ring. It was a tin object, superb, fine, grotesque, and hideous. Above all hideous: it assaulted love in its darkest, most basic regions. A veritable sexual shriek.

Of course, the artist who fashioned it was also inspired by visions of the wax museum. The stone of the ring, which was a simple piece of glass melted to the thickness of a lens, wholly resembled the magnifying glasses in the dioramas of the wax museum, in which I used to gaze at sunken ships enlarged to the extreme, battles against the Turks and the assassinations of royalty. On the ring could be seen a bouquet of flowers chiselled in tin or in lead and coloured with all the violent hues of the paintings in the dioramas.

The violet of throttled cadavers next to the pornographic red of women's garters, the leaden pallor of furious waves within a macabre light, like the semi-obscurity of funeral vaults covered with a pane of glass. All these framed by little brass leaves and mysterious signs. Hallucinatory.

Otherwise, I used to be impressed by everything that was an imitation. Artificial flowers, for example, and funeral wreaths, especially funeral wreaths, forgotten and dusty in their oval glass cases in the cemetery chapel, framing with old-fashioned delicacy anonymous old names, submerged in an unechoing eternity.

The cut-out pictures with which children play and the cheap statuettes from flea markets. In time, these statuettes would lose a head or an arm and their owners, repairing them, would surround the delicate throat with the white scurf of plaster. The bronze of the rest of the statuette would then acquire the significance of a tragic but noble suffering. And then there are the life-size Jesuses in Catholic churches. The stained glass windows cast into the altar the last reflections of a russet sunset, while the lilies at that hour exhale at the feet of Christ the plenitude of their heavy, lugubrious perfume. In this atmosphere full of ethereal blood and scented dizziness, a pale young man plays the final strains of a despairing melody on the organ.

All these things emigrated into life from the wax museum. In the dioramas of a fair I rediscover the shared space of all these nostalgias scattered through the world, which gathered altogether form its very essence.

A single and supreme desire remains alive for me: to witness the incineration of a wax museum; to see the slow and scabrous melting of the waxwork figures, to gaze petrified as the yellow and beautiful legs of the bride in the glass case writhe in the air and a real flame catches hold between the thighs, burning her sex.

5

Besides the wax museum, the August fair brought me many other occasions for sadness and exaltation. Its sweeping theatrical performance would swell like a symphony. It commenced with the prelude of isolated dioramas, which arrived much earlier than all the rest and set the general tone for the fair, like the scattered and drawn-out notes that announce at the beginning of the concerto the theme of the composition as a whole. The grandiose finale, on closing day, was an explosion of shouts, firecrackers and brass bands, followed by the immense silence of the deserted field.

The few dioramas that came early comprised, in essence, the fair as a whole and represented it with exactitude. It was sufficient for only the first of them to set up in order for the entire colouring, the entire sparkle and the entire carbide odour of the fair as a whole to seep down into the town.

From the throng of everyday sounds a thrum would suddenly detach itself, which was neither the creaking of tin, nor the far-off clinking of a bunch of keys, nor the drone of an engine: a sound easily recognisable among a thousand others, that of the "Wheel of Fortune".

In the obscurity of the boulevard a diadem of coloured sparks would then kindle, like the earth's first constellation. Soon others would follow it and the boulevard became a luminous corridor, along the length of which I walked petrified, just like I had once seen a boy of my age, in an illustrated edition of Jules Verne, leaning up against the window of a submarine, peering outside into the sub-oceanic darkness, into the wonderful, mysterious, marine phosphorescence.

A few days later the fair was in place. The semi-circle of booths was laid out, complete, and all at once became definitive.

Well-defined zones divided it into regions of shadows and lights – the same every year. There was, first of all, the string of restaurants with dozens of necklaces of coloured lights, then the dioramas with their freaks, the façade of the circus, drunken with light, and, finally, the obscure and lowly booths of the photographers. The crowd wheeled round, passing one after another areas of maximum illumination and regions of darkness, like the moon in my geography book, which alternately traversed typographical zones of black and white.

Above all we would enter the small and poorly lit booths, with few performers, lacking even a roof, where my father could negotiate at the entrance a reduced, group fee with the director, for our entire, numerous family.

The whole performance there would have something makeshift and uncertain about it. The cold night breeze blew over the audience's heads and on high, all the stars gleamed glassily in the sky above us. We were lost in a fairground booth, astray in the chaos of night, in the minuscule point of a planet in space. In that point, on that planet, people and dogs were performing on a stage; people were tossing various objects into the air and catching them, dogs were leaping through hoops and walking on their hind paws. Where were all these things taking place? The sky above us seemed even vaster...

On one occasion, in one of those impoverished booths, an artiste offered the audience a prize of five thousand lei to anyone who could imitate the sensational and very simple act he was about to perform. There were only five persons sitting on the audience benches. A fat gentleman, whom I had long known as a peerless miser, astonished by this unheard-of chance to win such an enormous sum in a mere fairground booth, quickly changed places, moving a number of benches closer to the stage, determined to follow with the most exacting attention the performer's every move, so that he could then reproduce them and win the prize.

There followed a few moments of terrible silence.

The artiste came to the edge of the stage: "Gentlemen", he said hoarsely, "I am about to blow cigarette smoke out of my throat". He lit a cigarette and taking his hand from his collar, where he had been holding it all the while, he blew fine trails of bluish smoke through the orifice of an artificial larynx, with which he had presumably been fitted following an operation. The gentleman on the front benches was left bewildered and embarrassed: his face turned red as far as the ears and returning to his former place he muttered loudly, through gritted teeth: "Well, of course, it's no wonder, if he has a contraption in his throat!"

The artiste replied imperturbably from the stage:

"Well, well, be my guest", perhaps truly disposed to grant the prize to any fellow sufferer...

In such booths, to earn their daily bread, pale and haggard old men would swallow stones and soap before the audience, young girls would contort their bodies, and anaemic and emaciated children, laying aside the corncobs they were nibbling, would climb onto the stage and dance, shaking bells tied to sticks.

In the daytime, immediately after lunch, in the blazing heat of the sun, the desolation of the fair was boundless. The immobility of the wooden fairground horses, with their boggling eyes and bronzed manes, somehow acquired the terrible melancholy of petrified life. From the booths came a warm smell of food, while a lone hurdy-gurdy, somewhere in the distance, insisted on pouring out its wheezing waltz, out of whose chaos, from time to time, would spurt a metallically whistling note, like a sudden "jet d'eau", high and slender, spouting from the mass of a water basin.

I used to like to linger for hours in front of the photographers' booths, contemplating the unknown persons, in groups or alone, petrified and smiling, in front of grey landscapes with cataracts and distant mountains. All these personages, due to their common backdrop, seemed members of the same family on an excursion to the same picturesque place, where they had been photographed one after another.

On one occasion, in such a display case, I came across my own photograph. That sudden encounter with myself, immobilised in a fixed attitude, there at the edge of the fair, had a depressing effect upon me.

Before arriving in my town, it had, of course, also travelled through other places unknown to me. In an instant I had the sensation of not existing except in a photograph. This inversion of mental positions often happened to me in the most divers circumstances. It would sneak up on me and all of a sudden transform my body from within. In an accident on the street, for example, I gazed for a number of minutes at what was happening as though at a hackneyed performance. All of a sudden, however, the entire perspective changed and – as in that game which consists in descrying a bizarre animal in the paint on the walls, which one day we can no longer find, because we see in its place, made up of the same decorative elements, a statue, a woman or a landscape – in that street accident, although everything remained intact, it was suddenly as if I was the one who was lying stretched on the ground and saw everything from my position as the person knocked down, from below, from the centre to the periphery, and with the vivid sensation of the blood trickling out of me. Likewise, without any effort, as a logical consequence of the mere fact that I was looking, I used to imagine myself in the cinema, experiencing the intimacy of the scenes on the screen. And it was exactly in this way that I saw myself in front of the photographer's booth, from the position of the one peering unflinchingly from the cardboard.

The whole of my life, the life of the one standing in the flesh and blood outside the glass display case, all of a sudden appeared to me indifferent and insignificant, just as to the living person behind the glass the voyage of his photographic 'I' through unknown towns also appears absurd.

In the same way in which the photograph that represented me wandered from place to place contemplating through the grimy and dusty pane of glass vistas that were ever new, so too I, on this side of the glass, forever perambulated a personage similar to myself from place to place, forever looking at new things and forever unable to understand anything of them. The fact that I moved, that I was alive, could be nothing more than a mere occurrence, an occurrence that had no meaning, because, just as I existed on this side of the glass display, I could also exist on the other side, with the same pale face, with the same eyes, with the same lustreless hair, all the things which in the mirror assembled me into a fleeing, bizarre, incomprehensible figure.

It was thus that there came from the exterior various warnings, immobilising me and abruptly snatching me away from everyday comprehension. They stupefied me, rooted me to the spot, and summed up in an instant the whole of the world's pointlessness.

Everything appeared to me in that instant chaotic, just as when listening to a brass band and stopping my ears and then ungluing my fingers for an instant, the music would seem in that instant pure noise.

I would wander through the fair all day and especially through the surrounding field, where the artistes and freaks from the booths gathered around a cauldron of maize porridge. They were dishevelled and dirty, having descended from their beautiful stage sets and nocturnal existences as acrobats, bodiless women and mermaids into the promiscuous mush and irremediable wretchedness of their humanity. What had seemed admirable in front of the booths, untrammelled and even sumptuous, here, at the back, in the light of day, sank back into petty and uninteresting familiarity, the same as the rest of the world.

One day, I witnessed the funeral of the child of one of the itinerant photographers.

The doors of the diorama were wide open and inside, in front of a photographic backdrop, the open coffin lay across two chairs.

The canvas behind depicted a splendid park with Italianate terraces and marble columns.

In this dreamlike setting, the little corpse, with its hands folded across its chest, in festive apparel, with silver tinsel in the buttonholes, seemed submerged in ineffable beatitude.

The child's parents and various women were weeping in despair around the coffin, while outside the brass band from the big top, lent free of charge by the director, was solemnly intoning a serenade from the "Intermezzo", the saddest passage in the programme.

In those moments, the dead body was of course unutterably happy and tranquil, in the intimacy of its profound peace, in the endless silence of the park with the plane trees.

Soon, however, it was torn from the solemnity in which it lay and loaded into a cart to be taken to the cemetery, to the cold damp grave allotted to it.

The park remained behind it, desolate and empty. At the fair, death too borrowed artificial and nostalgic settings, as though the fair itself formed a world apart, whose purpose was to demonstrate the infinite melancholy of artificial ornaments, from life's beginning until its end, and with the vivid example of pale existences, consummated in the sifted light of the wax museum, or in the room with an unbounded wall, lost in the super-terrestrial beauties of the photographers' backdrops.

For me, the fair thus became a desert island, laved by desolate auras, altogether similar to the indistinct and nevertheless limpid world into which my childhood crises bore me.

6

The upper floor of the Weber house, where I often went, after the death of old Etla Weber, resembled a genuine *Panoptikum*, a museum of curiosities. In rooms that were sunlit all the afternoon, the dust and the heat floated the length of glass cabinets full of old-fashioned things, cast onto the shelves at random. The beds had been moved to the ground floor and the rooms had remained empty. Old Samuel Weber (agency and commission) together with his two sons, Paul and Ozy, now lived in the rooms below.

In the first room, facing the street, the office had remained intact. It was a room that reeked of mould, crammed with ledgers and envelopes containing cereal samples, the walls plastered with old flyblown advertisements.

A few of these, pasted on the walls for many years, had been wholly integrated into the family life. Above the cash register, there was an advertisement for mineral water, presented by a tall, slender woman in diaphanous veils, pouring out the salutary remedy for the invalids at her feet. Of course, in the secret hours of the night Ozy Weber, too, would come to drink from the miraculous source, his gibbous chest jutting beneath his clothes like the distended sternum of a turkey.

The other family advertisement was for a transportation company and – with its ship gliding over ruffled waves – it rounded off the person of Samuel Weber, and thereby lent his captain's cap and thick-lens spectacles even more of a seagoing air. When old man Samuel used to shut the till of a cash register, pulling down on the iron lever, it really did seem as if he were turning the wheel at the helm of a ship on unknown seas. The pink cotton wool with which he stopped up his ears used to dangle in long fibrils and this was, of course, a wise precaution against the sea breezes.

In the second room, Ozy used to read pulp novels, sunk in a leather armchair, holding the book up very high for it to catch the faint light that came through the office from the street. In the gloom of a corner gleamed the skirt of a monumental tin spittoon in the form of a cat, and on the wall a mirror queerly reflected a square of grey light, like a phantom reminiscence of the day outside.

I used to come to see Ozy, like a dog entering a stranger's yard because the gate is open and no one drives it away. What drew me above all was a bizarre game. I do not know which of us invented it or in what circumstances. The game consisted of imaginary dialogues delivered with the utmost seriousness. We had to remain grave to the very end and not reveal in any way the non-existence of the things about which we were talking.

I would enter and Ozy would tell me in a dreadfully dry voice, without lifting his eyes from his book:

"The amidopyrine I took last night to make me sweat has provoked a dreadful cough. I tossed and turned in the sheets until daybreak. In the end... Matilda" – there was no Matilda – "came and gave me a massage".

The absurdity and stupidity of the things Ozy used to string together would hit me in the head like hammer blows. Perhaps I ought to have left the room forthwith, but with the minor voluptuousness of deliberately bringing myself down to his level I would answer in the same tone. I think this was the secret of the game.

"I have caught a chill, too", I would say (it was July), "and Dr Caramfil" – he was real – "has given me a prescription. A pity about the doctor... you know, this morning they arrested him..."

Ozy lifted his eyes from the book.

"You see, I have been telling you for a long time that he forges banknotes..."

"Well, of course", I added, "where else would he have got so much money to spend on showgirls at the cabaret?"

There was in those words first of all the rather sickly pleasure of submerging myself in the mediocrity of that dialogue and at the same time a vague impression of freedom. In this way I could slander at will the doctor, who lived nearby and about whom I knew that he went to bed at nine o'clock every evening.

In this way, we used to talk about anything at all, mixing real with imaginary things, until the whole conversation took on a kind of ethereal independence. It would float through the room, detached from us, like a curious bird. The existence of this bird was wholly external, and had it really appeared among us, we would have no more doubted it than we doubted the fact that our words were unconnected with us.

When I went out into the street once more, I would have the sensation of having slept profoundly. But the dream would seemingly always continue and I would look in astonishment at people talking seriously among themselves. Did they not realise that it is possible to speak gravely about anything at all, about absolutely anything at all?

Sometimes, Ozy would not be in the mood for conversation and then he would take me with him to rummage around the first floor. In the few years since it had been abandoned, and thanks to old man Weber's habit of sending all objects of no further use "upstairs", the most divers and extraordinary things had accumulated there.

In the rooms the scorching sun streamed through the dusty windows, which were without curtains. The glass cabinets rattled slightly as we trod the old floorboards, as if chattering their teeth. Between two of the rooms, a curtain of beads served as a door.

I would come from downstairs slightly dizzy from the heat of the day. The consummate desolation of the rooms would end up disturbing me. It was as if I had existed in a familiar world long ago, which I could now no longer very well recall. My body would have a bizarre stinging sensation of detachment. This sensation used to become more profound when I had to pass between the two rooms separated by the bead curtain.

In the drawers I used to seek above all old correspondence, in order to peel the stamps from the envelopes. From the yellowed packets would emerge a cloud of dust and mites, which would scurry to find shelter among the sheets of paper. A letter would fall to one side and open, revealing old-fashioned, intricate handwriting, with faded ink. There would be something sad and resigned in it, a kind of weary coda to the lapse of time since it had been written, a gentle slumber in eternity, like that of funeral wreaths. I also used to find old-fashioned photographs, with ladies wearing crinoline, or meditative gentlemen with their fingers touching their temples, smiling anaemically. At the bottom of the photograph there would be two angels carrying a basket of fruit and flowers, beneath which was inscribed *porte visite* or *souvenir*. Among the photographs and the objects in the glass cabinets – the pink glass fruit bowl with fluted edges, velvet handbags in which there was nothing but moth-eaten silk, various objects with unfamiliar monograms – among all these things there reigned an air of perfect understanding. It was like a life of their own, identical to the life of former times, when the photographs, for example, corresponded to persons who lived and breathed, and when the letters were written by genuine, warm hands. But it was a life reduced to a smaller scale, in a more restricted space, within the limits of the letters and the photographs, like in a stage set viewed through the thick lenses of a pair of binoculars, a stage set intact in all its components, except minuscule and distant.

Towards evening, when I descended, I would often meet on the stairs Paul Weber, who kept his wardrobe of clothes upstairs, in the first room, and who would be coming up to change.

He was a red-haired lad, with large hands and ruffled hair. He had large, thick lips and a clown-like nose. But in his eyes there floated an ineffably calm and restful candour. Everything Paul did possessed for this reason a detached and indifferent air.

I loved him very much, but in secret, and my heart would pound when I met him on the stairs. I liked the simplicity with which he used to speak to me, always smiling, as if our conversation had, besides its proper meaning, another more faraway and ephemeral sense. He would preserve that smile during the gravest conversations and even when he was discussing various business matters with old man Weber. I also loved Paul for the secret life he led beyond everyday pursuits and which reached me only in the rumours whispered in stupefaction by the grown-ups around me. Paul used to spend the money he earned on women at the variety theatre. There was in his debauchery an irremediable fatality, against which old man Weber struck as though a wall. On one occasion, the whole town was abuzz with the rumour that Paul had unharnessed the horses from the carriages in the square and brought them to the variety hall, where he had improvised a kind of circus, with the collusion of the town's most eminent drunkards. On another occasion it was rumoured that he had bathed with a woman in champagne. How many things did they not say about him?

It was impossible for me to define my sympathy towards Paul. I saw the people around me all too well, I saw all too well the pointlessness and boredom in which they consumed their lives: the young girls in the park laughing stupidly; the merchants with wily self-important eyes; my father's theatrical need to play the part of father; the cruel weariness of the beggars asleep in filthy corners; all these merged into a general and banal outward appearance, as though the world, such as it was, had long been waiting within me, constructed in its definitive form, while I, every day, did nothing more than verify its senescent contents in me.

All things were simple; Paul was outside them, in a density of life that was compact and absolutely inaccessible to my understanding.

Deep within me I preserved his every gesture and most fleeting attitude, not as a memory but rather as a double of their existence. Many times I would wrack myself to walk like him, I would study a certain gesture and copy it in front of the mirror until I thought I could repeat it exactly.

On the first floor of the Weber house, Paul was the most enigmatic, the finest of the waxwork figures. Soon, he brought there a pale woman, with the gestures and gait of a silent, missing mechanism...

The first floor thus completed its cabinet of curiosities, from Samuel Weber, the ship's captain, to the delicate and crippled phenomenon of the infantile Ozy.

7

Old junk and objects full of melancholy I also found on another abandoned upper floor, in the house of my grandfather. The walls here were covered with queer paintings, with thick, gilded wooden frames or thinner frames of red felt. There were also picture frames made of joined-together little shells, fashioned with a meticulousness that made me contemplate them for hours. Who had glued the shells together? What had been the living, minute gestures that had combined them? In such defunct workmanship entire lives were reborn, lives lost in the mist of time like images in two parallel mirrors, sunken in the greenish depths of a dream.

In one corner lay a gramophone with a lopsided funnel, beautifully painted in yellow and pink stripes, like an enormous portion of vanilla and rose ice cream, and on the table were to be found various coloured engravings, of which two depicted King Carol I and Queen Elisabeta.

Those engravings intrigued me for a long time. It seemed to me that the artist had great talent, because the facial features were very accomplished and fine, but I could not understand why he had worked with a grey, washed-out watercolour, as if the paper had been kept in water for a long time.

One day, I made an astonishing discovery: what I took to be faded pigment was nothing other than an agglomeration of minuscule letters, decipherable only with a magnifying glass.

In the whole drawing there was not a single pencil or brush stroke; everything was a conglomeration of words which told the life story of the King and Queen.

My astonishment all at once overturned the incomprehension with which I had been looking at the drawings. In the place of my mistrust toward the draughtsman's art, a boundless admiration was born.

In it I felt the misfortune of not having observed earlier the essential quality of the engraving and at the same time there grew in me my great mistrust in all that I saw: since I had contemplated for so many years the drawings without discovering the very matter of which they were composed, might it not be possible due to a similar myopia for the meaning of all the things around me to elude me, a meaning inscribed in them perhaps as clearly as the component letters of the pictures?

Around me, the surfaces of the world all of a sudden took on the strange glint and ambiguous opacity of curtains, opacities that become pellucid and all of a sudden reveal to us the depths of a room when a light is lit behind them.

Behind objects no light was ever lit, however, and they forever remained bathed by the volumes that hermetically sealed them, and which sometimes seemed to grow thinner in order to allow their true meaning to show through.

*

The upper floor also had other curios that belonged only there. For example, there was the view of the street as seen through the windows at the front.

The walls of the house being very thick, the windows were set deeply within them, forming alcoves in which one could sit very comfortably.

I used to install myself in one of them, as though in a little glass chamber, and open the windows onto the street.

The intimacy of the alcove as well as the pleasure of gazing at the street from such a pleasant vantage point would give me the idea of a vehicle to match, with soft cushions in which I could curl up, with windows through which I could view various unknown towns and landscapes, as the vehicle traversed the world.

On one occasion, I asked my father, who was recounting to me some memories from childhood, what had been his most ardent secret desire and he answered that he had wished above all to possess a miraculous vehicle in which he could curl up and which would convey him throughout the world.

I knew that in childhood he used to sleep on the upper floor with the windows onto the street and I asked him whether he used to like curling up in the alcoves of the windows, in order to gaze below.

He answered in astonishment that every evening when he went upstairs to bed he did indeed climb into an alcove and stay there for hours on end, so that he would often fall asleep there. His dream about the vehicle had probably come to him in the same place and in exactly the same circumstances as it had to me.

Thus there existed in the world not only cursed places that secreted vertigo and dizziness, but also other more benevolent spaces, from whose walls seeped pleasant and beautiful images.

The walls of the alcove filtered the dream of a vehicle that traversed the world and whoever lay curled up in that place was slowly imbued with the same idea as though by the dizzying smoke of hashish…

The upper floor also had two attics, of which one had a skylight. I used to climb through the skylight onto the roof of the house. The whole town spread around me, grey and amorphous, as far as the fields in the distance, where minuscule trains crossed a bridge as fragile as a plaything.

What I wanted was above all not to feel any vertigo and to achieve a feeling of equilibrium equal to that which I had on the ground below. I wanted to lead my "normal" life up on the roof and to be able to move in the rarefied, sharp air of the heights without fear and without any particular impression of emptiness. I used to think that if I managed this thing, in my body I would have felt elastic, ethereal counterweights, which would have wholly transformed me and made me into a kind of birdman.

I was convinced that it was only my anxiety not to fall that weighed me down and the thought that I was at a great height permeated me like a pain I would have liked to tear out by the root.

So that nothing would seem exceptional to me up there, I used to force myself every time to do something precise and banal: to read, to eat, or to sleep.

I would take the cherries and bread my grandfather gave me and climb up onto the roof with them. I would divide each cherry into quarters and eat them one at a time so that my "normal" occupation would last as long as possible. When I finished one, I would try with all my might to toss the pit into a large cauldron on display in front of a shop in the street below.

As soon as I came down, I would rush there to see how many seeds had hit their target. There were always three or four in the cauldron. What used to puzzle me exceedingly was that around the cauldron I would find no more than another three or four seeds. I had therefore eaten very few cherries, whereas to me it used to seem that I had been up on the roof for hours. In my grandfather's room, on the green faience face of the clock, I would likewise ascertain that no more than a few minutes had passed since I had climbed onto the roof. Time probably became denser and denser the higher up it "was spent". In vain did I seek to prolong it, staying up on the roof for as long as possible. Once I was down below, I always had to acknowledge that much less time had passed than I had imagined. This reinforced my strange feeling, on the ground, of the indefinite, of the interminable… Time here below was thinner than in reality, it contained less matter than at an altitude and thereby participated in the fragility of all things, which around me seemed so dense and which were nevertheless so instable, ready at any moment to shed their meaning and provisory outlines in order to appear in the form of their exact existence…

*

…The upper floor disintegrated piece by piece, object by object, after my grandfather's death. He died in the poky, damp room in the yard where he had chosen to shelter in his old age and which he did not wish to leave except to make his final journey.

I used to go there to see him every day, as his death approached, and I would be present during the prayer of the dying, which he himself would recite, in an unsteady and emotionless voice, after he had dressed in his new white shirt, so that the prayer would be more solemn.

It was in that little room that I saw him a few days later, dead, laid out on a tin table for his final toilet. My grandfather had a brother, younger than him by a number of years, with whom he bore a striking resemblance: they both had the same perfectly round head, like a sphere, covered with bright white hair, the same lively and penetrating eyes, and the same beard, with sparse strands, like an alveolate froth .

This uncle requested of the family the honour of washing the dead man and, although old and frail, he set to work with great zeal.

He was trembling from head to foot, as he fetched from the faucet in the yard buckets of water to heat in the kitchen.

When the water was heated, he took it into the little room and began to wash the corpse with clothes soap and a straw brush.

As he was scrubbing, he chewed teardrops between his teeth and – as if grandfather could have heard what he was saying – he spoke to him in a whisper, sighing bitterly: "This is the day I have come to… this is where all my black days have brought me… you are dead now and I am washing you… woe is me… that I had to live so long… long enough to catch this sad moment…"

With the sleeve of his coat he wiped his cheeks and his beard, damp with tears and sweat, and went on washing with even more zeal.

The two old men, astonishingly alike, one dead and the other washing him, formed a slightly hallucinatory picture. The men from the cemetery, who as a rule used to perform this duty, were standing in a corner and gazing spitefully at this intruder who was taking away their trade. They spoke among themselves in whispers, smoking and spitting on the ground in every direction. After an hour of toil, grandfather's brother finished. The cadaver was stretched out on the table, face down.

"Have you quite finished?" someone from the group asked him, a little man with a ginger goatee, clicking his fingers irritably and full of malice.

"I have finished", answered the dead man's brother. "Now let us dress him…"

"Aha! You've finished, you say", said the little man once more, full of irony. "So you think you've finished? So you think that's the way to put a dead man in the ground? In a filthy state like this?"

The poor old man was left astonished, in the middle of the room, with a straw brush in his hand, looking at all of us in the room and imploring us with mute looks to come to his defence. He knew very well that he had washed the dead man carefully and he did not think he deserved such an insult.

"Well, now I'm going to show you that you oughtn't poke your nose in where you have no business…" went on the insolent little man, snatching from the old man's hand the straw brush, and hastening over to the table he inserted it with a rapid movement into the anus of the dead man and extracted from therein a thick piece of excrement…

"You see that you don't know how to wash a dead body?" he said. "Did you want to bury him with this muck inside him?"

Grandfather's brother was convulsed by a violent tremor and burst into tears…

The burial took place on a scorching hot summer's day: nothing sadder and more impressive than a burial in the full heat and light of the sun, when people and things seem slightly larger, in the vapour of the boiling heat, as though seen through a magnifying glass.

What else could people do on such a day than bury their dead?

In the heat and torpor of the air, their gestures seemed already to have been made hundreds of years ago, the same then as now, the same as forever. The damp grave sucked up the dead body into a chill and darkness that certainly pervaded him like a supreme happiness. The clods of earth thudded heavily onto the planks while the people in dusty clothes, sweating and weary, continued to live their imperious lives on earth.

8

A few days after grandfather's funeral, Paul Weber got married.

Paul was a little weary at the wedding, but he had preserved his smile; a sad, forced smile in which lay the beginning of a commitment.

In the stiff collar, open at the front, his bare red throat was moving queerly; his trousers were seemingly longer and narrower than usual; the tails of his coat dangled grotesquely, like those on a clown. Paul had condensed in himself all the solemn ridiculousness of the ceremony. It was I who embodied its most secret and intimate ridiculousness. I was the little, unnoticed clown.

At the back of the dark salon, the bride waited in her armchair on the plinth. Her white veils were drawn over her face and only when she turned beneath the canopy and raised them did I see Edda for the first time…

The tables for the guests stretched whitely in a single row in the yard; at the gate had gathered all the town's tramps; the sky had an indeterminate clayey yellow colour; pale misses in blue and pink silk dresses shared out small silvery bonbons. It was a wedding. The music was a scraping, sad old waltz; from time to time its rhythm swelled, burgeoned and seemed to become livelier, then the melody would thin out again, thinner and thinner, until all that remained was the metallic thread of a single flute.

A dreadfully long day; too much of a day for a wedding. No one came to the bottom of the yard, where the hotel stables were and a mound from which I gazed into the distance, while around me a few hens pecked grains among the blades of grass. From the yard wafted the sad waltz interwoven with the scent of damp hay from the stables. It was from there that I saw Paul doing something extraordinary: he was speaking with Ozy and of course he was telling him something amusing, perhaps a joke, because the cripple began to laugh, turned violet, almost suffocating beneath his bulging, starched shirt front.

Night came at last. The few trees in the yard were submerged in darkness, excavating from the blackness a mysterious and invisible park.

In the poorly lit salon the bride forever sat on the plinth next to Paul, inclining her head toward him when he said something to her in a whisper, her arm limp between his fingers, which caressed the length of her white glove.

A few cakes had been brought out onto the table. There was above all a monumental cake like a castle fortified with thousands of pink crème battlements and buttresses. The petals of the icing sugar flowers gleamed matte and oily. The knife was thrust into the centre of the cake and a rose creaked with a keen sound beneath the blade, shattering like glass into dozens of pieces. The old ladies strolled around majestically in their velvet dresses with countless jewels on their chests and fingers, advancing slowly and solemnly like the miniature altars of an ambulatory church, richly ornamented.

Slowly, slowly, the salon grew hazy and all I saw became hazier and more absurd… I fell asleep gazing at my red, boiling hands.

The room in which I awoke smelled of stale smoke. In a mirror in front of me the window reflected the dawn, which came into view like a perfect square of blue silk. I was lying on a rumpled bed, full of pillows. A thin sound was droning in my ears like inside a seashell; in the room the wispy smoke was still floating in layers.

I tried to get up and my fingers sank into the wooden carvings of the headboard; there were some that protruded and others that receded, burgeoning in the colourless light of the room, scooped out in thousands of crenelations, cavities, and crimped lichens. In a few seconds the room filled with all kinds of intangible volutes through which I had to pass in order to reach the door, brushing them aside in order to clear a path for myself. My head was droning and all the caverns of the air seemingly echoed this murmur. In the corridor the white light coldly bathed my cheeks and I fully woke up. I met a gentleman in a long nightshirt who gazed at me with a very annoyed air as if he were reproaching me for being dressed so early in the morning.

Further on, there was no one. Below in the yard the tables for the guests had remained, their pine boards now bare. The dawn was sullen and cold. The wind was blowing coloured bonbon wrappers around the yard. How had the bride held her head? How had she leaned it on Paul's shoulder? In some wax museums the mannequins of the women have a mechanism that makes them lean their head to one side and close their eyes.

The streets of the town had lost all meaning; the cold pierced through my coat; I was sleepy and cold. When I closed my eyes the wind pressed its colder cheek against mine and on the other side of my eyelids I could feel it like a mask, the mask of my face, inside of which it was dark and cold like behind a real metal mask. Which house in my path was about to explode? Which fencepost was about to twist like a rubber cosh to show it was grimacing at me? Nowhere in the world, and under no circumstances, did anything ever happen.

*

When I arrived in the market the men were unloading meat for the butchers' stalls. They were carrying in their arms crimson, lurid cattle, moist with blood, tall and proud, like dead princesses. In the air there was a warm scent of flesh and urine; the butchers were hanging up each cow head downward. Their bulging black eyes pointed at the floor. They were now lined up along the white porcelain walls like crimson sculptures hewn from the most various and tender matter, with the watery and prismatic glint of silks and the cloudy transparency of gelatine. At the edge of the open belly hung the lacework of muscles and the heavy, strung beads of fat. The butchers plunged their red arms inside and extracted the precious offal, which they laid out on a table: objects of flesh and blood, rotund, broad, elastic and warm.

The fresh meat glistened like the petals of monstrous, hypertrophied roses. The dawn turned as blue as steel; the cold morn resounded with a deep organ-pipe sound.

The carthorses regarded the people with their forever watery eyes; a mare released a boiling stream of urine onto the cobbles. In the puddle, frothy in places, clear in others, the sky was reflected, deep and black.

Everything became faraway and desolate. It was morning; the men were unloading the meat; the wind was piercing through my coat; I was shivering from the cold and from sleeplessness; in what kind of world did I live?

I began to run along the streets madly. The sun could be glimpsed red upon the rooftops. In the lanes with tall houses darkness still reigned and only at the intersections of the streets did the light gush glittering as if through open doors along the length of empty corridors.

I passed the back of Weber's house; the heavy shutters of the upper floor were closed; everything as deserted and sad; the wedding had finished.

9

The shadows and coolness of the upper floor of Weber's house were bathed in a different light with the arrival of Edda, just as the clearings in deep forests become more lambent due to a green light winnowed through leaves.

Edda first of all hung curtains in the windows and laid soft carpets on the floor, in which all the desolate echoes of the upper floor fell silent.

Every morning we would be up on the balcony making an inventory of the host of contorted and artificial objects that were emerging from the glass cabinets.

Together with Ozy, I would dust them conscientiously, only to cast them thereafter into a rubbish skip.

On the balcony, Edda would come and go, wearing a blue smock, with house slippers whose heels clacked at every step. She would sometimes remain leaning against the balustrade, partly shutting her eyelids and gazing at the brilliant sky.

The first floor acquired an ineffable perfume, which changed its content, like a strong essence mixed into a tincture of alcohol.

All events were thus destined to appear in my life jerkily and abruptly, incomprehensibly, isolated in their outlines from any past. Edda became one more additional object, a mere object whose existence tormented me and exasperated me, like a word repeated countless times, which becomes all the more meaningless the more its meaning seems imperiously necessary.

The world's perfection was about to shine through from somewhere, like a bud that must break through its final pellicle to feel the open air.

On summer mornings, on the balcony of the upper floor, something used to happen and my whole body would be wracked in vain to understand what exactly it was.

I was armed for an encounter with Edda, with all the disillusionments, all the humiliations, and all the ridiculousness required for an affair.

The bead curtain between the rooms had been kept. White lingerie with large coloured ribbons and bows had occupied the glass cabinets, and the Weber house had been wholly transformed. A pantomime with four characters commenced around Edda: Paul became solemn and faithful; old man Weber bought himself a new cap and gold-framed spectacles; Ozy would wait breathless with excitement for Edda to call him upstairs; and I would remain on the balcony, gazing with watery eyes into the emptiness.

Every Saturday afternoon, we used to gather in the room at the front, where the gramophone would play oriental arias from *Kismet*, and Edda would serve us bittersweet cakes made from honey and almonds. In a fruit bowl there were nuts, to which Samuel Weber in particular would help himself, gulping the mouthfuls intermittently and emphatically, so that his Adam's apple used to stretch up and down in his throat like a rubber doll.

He would sit cross-legged, which constituted a position of repose wholly outside business and cereals, something in the manner of actors on a theatre stage, and when he spoke he would pucker his lips so that his gold teeth would not show.

He was fearful to place his hand on even the smallest object, and when he passed through the bead curtain, he would turn around and slowly close the two halves, so as not to make a tinkle.

Paul alone strode over the carpets calmly and self-confidently. He made broad gestures in which there was nothing to add or subtract and when he took Edda in his arms, we, the other three, were, of course, satisfied, in the end, that he did so better than any of us.

As for myself, I do not very well know what used to go on during those days.

On one of those afternoons, sitting snugly in an armchair, I firmly pressed my head against the felt. The sparse prickles of velour embedded themselves in my face, which produced in me rather a lively pain. In an instant there grew in me, ridiculous and superb, an imperious desire for heroism, and the most various and absurd thoughts, such as can gush forth only on a Saturday afternoon, in the tedium of gramophone music.

I buried my head in the felt harder and harder and, as the pain became more violent, my endurance became all the more tenacious.

Perhaps in us there exist a hunger and a thirst different from those that are organic, and something in me needed then to slake itself with a simple and acute pain. Harder, ever harder, I buried my face and grated it against the harsh bristles, tormenting myself with a suffering that began to shatter me.

All of a sudden, Edda was left standing with a gramophone disk in her hands, looking at me in bewilderment. Around me a silence had descended, which embarrassed me exceedingly. "What can have got into him?" Edda asked. And I, too, saw myself, in the mirror. I was ridiculous, perfectly ridiculous: on my face a violet patch was oozing drops of blood.

My eyes wide open, my face bloodied, gazing in the mirror I could nevertheless not help but notice that I bore an allegorical resemblance to the cover of that fashionable novel that depicted the Tsar of the Russians, bloodied and holding his hand to his jaw, following an assassination attempt.

Much more than the pain of my face, what tormented me now was the miserable destiny of my heroism, which had ended up by acting out, in the flesh and blood, an episode from *Mysteries of the Petrograd Court*.

Edda soaked a handkerchief in medicinal alcohol and dabbed my cheek. I closed my eyes because of the stinging. The skin in that spot grown hot, burning like a flame.

I descended the stairs dizzily and the avid streets received me once more into their dust and monotony.

Summer had bloated the park, the trees and the air, chaotically, as though in the drawing of a lunatic.

All its vast and scorching blast had grown monstrously in the greenery, thick and overflowing.

The park had overflowed like lava; the stones were burning; my hands were red and heavy.

In that soft, hot desolation I saw the image of Edda, sometimes multiplied tenfold – ten, a hundred, a thousand Eddas – one next to another in the summer heat, statuesque, identical, obsessive.

There was in all this a cruel and lucid desperation, permeating everything I saw and felt. Parallel to my elementary and simple life, within me unfolded other intimacies, warm, beloved and secret, like a terrible, fantastical inner leprosy.

I used to compose the details of imaginary scenes with the most meticulous precision. I would see myself in hotel rooms, with Edda lying beside me, as the light of sunset seeped through the thick lace curtains, and their fine shadow etched its web on her sleeping face. I would see the pattern of the carpet by the bed, upon which rested her shoes, and her half-opened handbag on the table, out of which poked the corner of a handkerchief. The wardrobe with the mirror which reflected half of the bed and the floral stencils on the walls…

All these would leave me with a rather bitter aftertaste…

I used to follow strange women in the gardens, walking behind them, matching them step for step until they reached their homes, where I would remain standing in front of the closed door, disconsolate, despairing.

One evening, I walked a woman as far as the threshold of her home.

The house had a front garden, faintly illuminated by an electric bulb.

With a sudden, hitherto unsuspected urge, I opened the gate and stole into the garden behind the woman. Meanwhile, she had gone into the house without noticing me, and I remained alone, in the middle of the garden path. A strange idea entered my head…

In the middle of the garden there was a flowerbed. In an instant I was kneeling in the middle of it, with my hand to my heart. Exposed, I assumed an imploring position. This is what I wanted: to remain there for as long as possible, motionless, petrified in the middle of the flowerbed. I had long been wracked by the longing to commit an absurd act in a wholly strange place, and now it had come to me spontaneously, effortlessly, almost exaltedly. The evening hummed warmly around me and in the first moments I felt an enormous gratitude towards myself for the courage of having made this decision.

I intended to stay there completely motionless even if no one came to chase me away, even if I had to stay there until the next morning. Slowly, slowly, my legs and arms grew stiff and my posture acquired an inner shell of boundless calm and motionlessness.

How long did I remain there like that? All of a sudden I heard shouting in the house and the outside light went out.

In the darkness I could better feel the night breeze and the isolation in which I found myself, in the garden of a strange house.

A few minutes later, the light came back on and then it went out once more. Someone in the house was turning it on and off to see whether it would have any effect on me.

I remained motionless, determined to brave experiences even worse than the game with the light. I kept my hand to my chest and my knee to the earth.

The door opened and someone came out into the garden, while a deep voice from the house shouted: "Leave him, leave him be, he'll go away by himself". The woman whom I had followed came up to me. She was now wearing a housecoat and slippers, and her hair was unplaited. She looked me in the eyes and for a few seconds said nothing. We both remained silent. At last, she put her hand on my shoulder and said gently, "Come on… it's over now", as though she wanted me to understand that she had perceived my gesture and had remained silent for a while precisely in order to allow it to reach its own conclusion.

This spontaneous understanding disarmed me. I stood up and brushed the dust from my trousers. "Aren't your legs aching?" she asked me. "I wouldn't have been able to stay motionless for so long…" I wanted to say something but all I could manage was to mutter, "Good evening", and I left in haste.

All my desperations were now howling painfully within me once more.

10

I was a tall, thin, pale boy, with a slender throat poking from the overly large collar of my tunic. My long hands dangled below my jacket like freshly flayed animals. My pockets bulged with objects and bits of paper. I used to have a hard time retrieving a handkerchief from the bottom of these pockets to wipe the dust off my boots, when I reached the streets of the "centre".

Around me evolved the simple and elementary things of life. A pig would be scratching itself against a fence and I would stop for minutes at a time to watch it. Nothing surpassed in its perfection the rasping of coarse bristles against wood; I found in it something immensely satisfying, a soothing assurance that the world continued to exist...

On a street at the edge of town I found a workshop for rustic woodcarving, where, again, I used to linger for a long time.

In the shop there were thousands of smooth white things among the curly shavings that fell from the workbench and filled the room with their rigid froth, redolent of resin.

The piece of wood beneath the tool would grow finer, paler, and its capillaries would come into view limpidly and well inscribed, like those beneath a woman's skin.

Alongside, on a table there were wooden balls, calm and massy balls that filled the whole surface area of my hand with a smooth, ineffable weight.

Then there were the wooden chess pieces, redolent of fresh wood stain, and the entire wall covered with flowers and angels.

Such materials sometimes exuded sublime patches of eczema, with lacework suppurations, painted or carved.

In winter, blisters of rime erupted, the solidified water acquiring carven forms. In summer flowers gushed forth in thousands of minuscule explosions, with red, blue and orange petalised flames.

Throughout the year the master carver, with his spectacles missing one lens, would extract from the wood spirals of smoke and Red Indian arrows, seashells and ferns, peacock feathers and human ears.

In vain did I watch that slow labour in order to catch the moment when the ragged, moist piece of wood exhaled itself in a petrified rose.

In vain did I myself try to consummate such a miracle. I held in my hand an untrimmed, ruffled, stony piece of pinewood, but from beneath the plane, all of a sudden, there emerged something as slippery as a fainting fit.

Perhaps, as I began to plane the plank, I was overcome by a deep sleep and extraordinary powers then spread their tentacles through the air, entering the wood and producing the cataclysm.

Perhaps the whole world came to a stop in those few seconds and no one was aware of the time elapsed. In deep sleep the craftsman had of course carved all the lilies on the walls and all the violins with their volutes.

When I awoke, the plank revealed to me the lines of its age, like a palm shows the lines of fate.

I picked up one object after another and their variety dizzied me. In vain did I grip a file, slowly run my fingers over it, place it to my cheek, swivel it, let it fall spinning to the floor… In vain… in vain… nothing had any meaning.

Everywhere, hard, inert matter surrounded me – here in the form of wooden balls and carvings – in the street in the form of trees, houses, and stones; immense and futile, matter enveloped me from head to foot. In whichever direction my thoughts turned, matter surrounded me, from my clothes to the springs in the forest, passing through walls, trees, stones, glass…

Into every cranny the lava of matter had spilled from the earth, petrifying in the empty air, in the form of houses with windows; trees with branches that ever rose to pierce the emptiness; flowers, soft and colourful, which filled the small curved volumes of space; churches whose cupolas soared ever higher, as far as the slender cross at their pinnacle, where matter halted its trickling into the heights, powerless to ascend further.

Everywhere, matter had infested the air, irrupting into it, filling it with the encysted abscesses of stones, with the wounded hollows of trees…

I went maddened by the things I saw, things I was destined not to be able to escape.

Nevertheless, I would sometimes chance to find an isolated spot where I could allow my head to rest at will. There for a moment all the vertigo would fall silent and I would feel better.

On one occasion I found such a refuge in the strangest and most unsuspected place in the town.

It was indeed so bizarre that I myself would never have imagined that it might provide such a lonely and admirable den.

I think it was only this burning thirst to fill the void of the days, howsoever and wheresoever, that impelled me to this new adventure.

One day, passing in front of the variety theatre in the town, I plucked up the courage to enter.

It was a tranquil, luminous afternoon. I crossed a grubby courtyard with a number of closed doors. At the bottom, I found one that was open, leading to a staircase.

In the hall a woman was washing clothes. The passage smelled of lye. I climbed the stairs and the woman did not say anything to me at first, and then, when I was halfway up, she turned her head to me and muttered, more to herself, "Aha! So you've come..." obviously mistaking me for a familiar person.

When, long after this occurrence, I recalled this detail, the woman's words did not seem quite so simple: in them there was perhaps the announcement of a fatality that presided over my restlessness and which through the mouth of the washerwoman revealed to me that the places of my adventures were fixed in advance and that I was destined to fall into them like well-laid traps. "Aha! You have come", said the voice of destiny, "you have come because you had to come, because you could not escape..."

I reached a long corridor, strongly heated by the sun that streamed through all the windows overlooking the yard.

The doors of the rooms were closed; no sound could be heard anywhere. In one corner a tap dripped continuously. It was hot and deserted in the corridor, and the drain slowly imbibed each droplet of water as if it were sipping a drink that was too cold.

At the bottom, a door led to an attic, where I found some clothes hanging on washing lines. I crossed the attic and came to a small hall with clean, freshly whitewashed rooms. In each of them could be found a chest and a mirror; they were of course the dressing rooms of the variety artistes.

On one side, there was a ladder, by which I descended onto the stage of the theatre.

Thus, all of a sudden, I found myself on the empty stage, in front of the deserted auditorium. My footfalls had a strange resonance. All the chairs and tables were arranged properly, as for a performance. I found myself in front of them, alone on the stage, in the middle of a theatre set depicting a forest.

I wanted to open my mouth, sensing that I had to say something aloud, but the silence turned me to marble.

All of a sudden I espied the prompter's booth. I bent down and looked inside.

In the first few seconds I could not make anything out, but gradually I discovered the basement below the stage, full of broken chairs and old props.

With very cautious movements I thrust myself into the aperture and climbed down beneath the stage.

The dust had settled everywhere in thick layers. In a corner there lay stars and crowns made of gilded cardboard, which must have served for a fairytale scene. In another corner there was some rococo-style furniture, a table, and some chairs with broken legs. In the middle there was a solemn, high-backed chair, something like a royal throne.

I sank into it, exhausted. At last, I found myself in a neutral space, where no one could be aware of me. I rested my hands on the gilded arms of the throne and let myself be lulled by the pleasant sensation of solitude.

The darkness around me had dispersed a little; filthy and dusty, the light of day streamed through a few double windows. I was far from the world, far from the hot and exasperating streets, in a cool and secret cell, at the bottom of the earth. The silence floated on the old and mouldering air.

Who could have suspected where I was? It was the most unusual place in town and I felt a calm joy thinking about how I was there.

Around me lay crooked armchairs, dusty beams and abandoned objects: it was the very place where all my dreams intersected.

Thus I remained, tranquil, in consummate beatitude, for a few hours.

At last, I abandoned the hideaway, following the same route whence I had come. Curiously, I did not meet anyone this time either.

The corridor seemed ablaze, in the flames of the setting sun. The drain continued to imbibe water with small and regular sips.

In the street, I had the impression that none of this had happened. But my trousers were full of dust and I left them like that, without wiping them, as a ready-to-hand proof of the faraway and admirable intimacy I had abandoned beneath the stage.

The next day, at the same hour of the afternoon, I was all of a sudden overcome with nostalgia for the isolated basement.

It was almost certain that this time I would meet someone, either in the corridor, or in the auditorium. For a while I tried to resist the temptation to go there once more. But I was too weary, too hot from the heat of the day, for the possibility of a risk to frighten me. Come what may, I had to return below the stage once more.

I entered by the same door in the courtyard and climbed the same flight of stairs. The corridor was as deserted as before and there was no one in the attic or in the auditorium below.

In a few minutes, I was once more in my place, on the theatrical throne, in my delicious solitude. My heart was thudding; I was exceedingly excited by the extraordinary success of my escapade.

I began to stroke the arms of the throne ecstatically. I would have liked the situation in which I found myself to penetrate me as deeply as could be, to weigh within me as heavily as could be, to permeate every fibre of my body so that I could feel that it was verisimilar.

This time, too, I remained for a long time and left once more without meeting anyone…

I began to come regularly, spending every afternoon beneath the stage.

As though it were perfectly normal, the corridors were always empty. I would sink into the throne, shattered by the beatitude. The same cool, blue cellar light streamed through the filthy windows. The same secret atmosphere of consummate solitude reigned, of which I could never have my fill.

Those daily excursions to the theatre basement came to an end one afternoon as strangely as they had begun.

As I was emerging from the attic at twilight, in the corridor a woman was fetching water from the standpipe.

I passed her slowly, at the risk of being asked what I was doing there. However, she went on with her business, with the indifferent and defensive air that women assume when they suspect a stranger wishes to talk to them.

At the top of the stairs, I stopped, now wishing to strike up conversation with her. There existed, on the one hand, my hesitation, and, on the other, the woman's sulky certainty that I was going to speak to her. The gurgle of water from the tap coldly divided the silence into two well-defined domains.

I turned around and approached her. It came into my head to ask her whether she knew any person who might pose for me as a life model for some drawings. I uttered the word "person" with a perfectly nonchalant air, so that in it could not be glimpsed any vulgar urge merely to see a woman naked, but rather my wholesome and abstract preoccupation with sketching.

A few days previously, a student, in order to bait me, of course, had said that in Bucharest he called young women to his house under the pretext of sketching them and then slept with them. I was sure that none of this was true and I sensed, I do not know how, in the student's story the awkwardness of a tale he had heard from someone else and then retold on his own account. It had, however, remained firmly imprinted on my mind and now there arose a wonderful opportunity to apply it. In this way, an occurrence involving a distant stranger, having crossed the unfertile terrain of another, became once more ripe enough to fall back into reality.

The woman did not understand, or pretended she did not understand, although I strove to explain things as clearly as possible.

As I was speaking, a door opened a little way and another woman came out.

They both consulted each other in a whisper.

"Well, we'll take you to Elvira, then: she doesn't have anything better to do", said one of them.

She led me to a low, dark little room next to the attic, which I had not noticed before. Inside, instead of a window, there were two holes in the wall, through which entered a cold draught. It was the cinema projection room, from where they projected films into the garden of the variety theatre. On the floor could be seen the marks left by the cement pedestal on which the apparatus had stood.

In a corner, a sick woman was languishing in bed, the blankets pulled up as far as the mouth, her teeth chattering. The other women went away and left me alone in the middle of the room.

I went over to the bed. The sick woman extended a hand from under the blanket and offered me it. It was a long, fine, frozen hand. I told her in a few words that there had been a mistake, and that I had been brought to her on account of a misunderstanding. I mumbled an apology, telling her vaguely what it was about: drawings for an art competition.

From all that I said she picked up on the word "competition" and replied in a dull voice: "Alright… alright… I'll give you the competition… when I get better… I haven't got anything now".

She had understood that I needed money. I gave up any other explanation and was left standing there in embarrassment for a few moments, not knowing how to make my exit.

In the meantime, she began to complain in a very natural tone of voice, as though she wanted to apologise for not giving me anything.

"You see, I have ice on my tummy… I'm hot… I'm hot… I'm very ill…"

I left, saddened, and I never went back to the variety theatre again.

11

Autumn came, with its red sun and misty mornings. The houses at the edge of town, jumbled together in the light, smelled of fresh whitewash. These were washed-out days with a cloudy sky like dirty laundry. The rain rattled infinitely in the deserted park. The thick curtains of water shimmered in the lanes as though in an immense auditorium. I trod through the wet grass and the water streamed down my hair and my arms.

In the filthy lanes at the edge of town, when the rain stopped, the doors would open and the houses inhaled the air. They were modest interiors with their lathed cupboards, with their bouquets of artificial flowers arranged on the commode, with their bronze-plated plaster statuettes and their photographs from America. Lives of which I knew nothing, lost in the slightly mouldy spaces of low-ceilinged rooms, sublime in their resigned indifference.

I would have liked to live in those houses, to imbue myself with their intimacy, allowing all reveries and all bitterness to dissolve in their atmosphere as though in a strong acid.

What would I have not given to be able to enter such and such a room, treading familiarly, slumping wearily on the old couch, among the floral cretonne cushions? To acquire there a different inner intimacy, to breathe a different air, and myself to become different, another... stretched on the couch to contemplate the street along which I was walking, from inside the house, from behind the curtains (and I would seek to imagine as precisely as possible how the street would look from the couch through the open door), to be able to find all of a sudden within me memories I had never experienced, memories belonging to the intimacy of the brass-plated statuettes and the old globular lampshade with its blue and violet butterflies.

How good I would have felt within the limits of that cheap and indifferent décor, which knew nothing of me...

In front of me the dirty lane forever spread its muddy mush. There were houses spread out like fans, others that were as white as sugar cubes, and others that were small, with roofs pulled down over their eyes, clenching their jaws like boxers. I would meet hay carts, or, all of a sudden, extraordinary things: a man in the rain, carrying on his back a candelabra with crystal ornaments, which tinkled like bells on the man's shoulders, while heavy drops of water trickled over all the gleaming facets. In what did the weight of the world ultimately reside?

The rain bathed the wilted flowers and plants in the park. Autumn kindled bronze, red and purple blazes in them, like flames that flare more brightly before they are quenched. In the market, water and mud flowed dishevelled from huge mounds of vegetables. In the slicing of the beetroots there would suddenly loom the red, dusky blood of the earth. Further on, sound, gentle potatoes lay next to the lopped heads of heaped cabbages. In a corner rose the mound of swollen and hideous pumpkins, of an exasperating beauty, their taut skin bursting with the plenitude of a sun drunken all summer long.

In the middle of the sky, the clouds bunched together and then unravelled, leaving between them narrow spaces like corridors lost in the boundlessness or else immense holes, which revealed better than anything else the agonising emptiness that forever floated above the town.

The rain would then fall from far away, from a sky that no longer had any bounds. I liked the altered colour of the damp wood and the rusty palings in front of prim, private gardens, through which the wind would pass mixed with the streaming water, swishing like the huge tail of a horse.

Sometimes I wanted to be a dog, to see that wet world from the oblique perspective of animals, from below, lifting my head. To move more closely to the ground, with my eyes fixed upon it, closely bound to the livid colour of the mud.

This desire, which had long lain within me, frenetically tumbled into that autumn day on the vacant lot...

*

That day, I had reached the edge of town on foot, arriving at the field of the cattle market.

In front of me stretched the rain-soaked vacant lot like an immense puddle of mud. The cowpats exhaled an acidic scent of urine. The sun was setting over a stage set with tatters of gold and dark red. In front of me the warm soft mud stretched into the distance. What else could bathe my heart in joy except this pure and sublime mass of filth?

At first I hesitated. In me there struggled the last traces of upbringing with the strength of dying gladiators. But in an instant they were plunged into black, opaque night, and I knew nothing more of myself.

I entered the mud first with one foot, then with the other. My boots slithered pleasingly in the elastic and sticky mulch. I was now a thing that had grown from the mud, I was one with it, as if I had sprouted from the earth.

I was now sure that the trees, too, were nothing more than congealed mud that had sprouted from the crust of the earth. Their colour said it well enough. And only the trees? What about the houses, the people? Above all, the people. All people. It was, of course, not a matter of the stupid legend about coming from the earth and returning to it, ashes to ashes and dust to dust . That was too vague, too abstract, too inconsistent compared with the muddy vacant lot. People and things had sprouted from the very cow clart and urine into which I was now thrusting very concrete boots.

In vain had people swathed themselves in silky white skin and arrayed themselves in clothes. In vain, in vain… In them slumbered mud, implacable, imperious and elementary; warm, thick, reeking mud. The boredom and stupidity with which they filled their lives also showed this well enough.

I myself was a special creation of the mud, a missionary it had sent into this world. In those moments I very well sensed how its memory was returning to me and I recalled my nights of tossing and turning, the hot darkness in which my essential mud surged impotently, struggling to reach the surface. Then I would close my eyes and continue to boil in the obscurity of meaningless murmurings…

Around me stretched the muddy vacant lot… This was my authentic flesh, flayed of clothes, flayed of skin, flayed of muscle, *flayed to the mud*.

Its elastic wetness and raw scent welcomed me into their depths, for I belonged to them as far as the very depths. A few, purely accidental appearances, such as, for example, the gestures I was capable of making, the thin, sleeked hair on my head, or my glassy, moistened eyes, separated me from its immobility and ancient filth. It was little, all too little, before the immense majesty of the mire.

I was walking in all directions. My feet sank as far as the ankles. It was drizzling and far away the sun was bedding down behind a curtain of bloody, purulent clouds.

All of a sudden I bent down and thrust my hands into the clart. Why not? Why not? I felt like shouting.

The ooze was warm and gentle; my hands slipped through it without resistance. When I clenched my fist, the mud was extruded through my fingers in beautiful glossy black slices.

What had my hands been doing up until then? Where had they been wasting their time? I had used to walk with them here and there, wherever my heart willed. What had they been up until then except poor imprisoned birds, tied to my shoulders by a terrible chain of skin and muscle? Poor birds destined to flutter in stupid well-mannered gestures, learned and rehearsed as things of worth.

Slowly, slowly, they grew wild once more and rejoiced in their ancient freedom. Now they were rolling their head in the clart, they were cooing like doves, beating their wings, happy… happy…

I joyously began to wave them over my head, allowing them to fly. Large drops of mud fell on my face and clothes.

Wherefore would I have wiped them? Wherefore? It was only a beginning; no grave consequence followed upon my deed, the sky did not tremble, the earth did not quake. I straightaway wiped a hand covered in filth across my face. An immense joy overcame me. It had been a long time since I had been so well disposed. I placed both hands to my face and throat, and then I rubbed my hair with them.

All of a sudden the rain began to fall more finely and more rapidly. The sun still lit the vacant lot like an immense lamp at the bottom of a grey marble hall. It was raining in the sunlight, a golden rain, redolent of fresh laundry.

The field was deserted. Here and there lay a heap of corncobs on which the cattle had been feeding. I took one and opened it carefully. I was shivering from the cold and with my muddied hands it was difficult to peel away the leaves. But this was interesting to me. There were so many things to be seen in a corncob. At a distance there was a hut with a thatched roof. I ran there and entered under the eaves. The roof was so low that I bumped my head against it. The earth by the wall was perfectly dry. I stretched out on the ground. I propped my head on some old sacks and, cross-legged, I could now freely give myself up to minute analysis of the corncob.

I was happy to be able to devote myself to this impassioned research. The runnels and indentations of the corncob filled me with enthusiasm. I broke it open with my teeth and found inside a downy, sweetish fluff. This lining was wonderful for a corncob; if people too had had arteries lined with downy fluff then the darkness in them would surely have been sweeter, more bearable.

I looked at the corncob and in me the silence laughed calmly. It was as if inside me someone had been lathering soapsuds.

It was raining and the sun was shining, and far away in the mist the town was steaming like a heap of garbage. A few roofs and church spires shone strangely in this damp gloaming. I was so happy that I did not know what absurd act to perform next: to analyse the corncob, to stretch my bones, or to gaze at the distant town.

Some distance away from my feet, where the mud began, a female frog suddenly made a few leaps. At first, it approached me, but then it suddenly changed its mind and headed towards the field. "Adieu, frog!" I called out behind her. "Adieu! My heart breaks at you leaving me so soon... Adieu, beautiful frog maiden!" I began to improvise a long speech addressed to this frog and when I finished speaking I threw the corncob at her, perhaps I would hit her...

At last, gazing up at the eaves, I closed my weary eyes and slept.

I was overwhelmed by deep sleep, to the marrow of my bones.

...I dreamed that I found myself on the streets of a dusty town, with strong sunlight and white houses; perhaps an oriental town. I was walking alongside a woman in black, dressed in mourning veils. Strangely, however, the woman did not have a head. The veils were very well arranged where her head should have been, but in its place there was nothing but a gaping hole, a spherical emptiness down to the nape.

We were both in a great hurry and one next to the other we were following a cart marked with red crosses in which lay the corpse of the husband of the woman in black.

I realised that it was in wartime. Indeed, we soon reached a railway station and descended a staircase into a basement lit dimly by an electric bulb. A convoy of wounded had just arrived and the nurses were swarming agitatedly up and down the platform, with baskets of cherries and bagels, which they shared out to the invalids in the train.

All of a sudden, from a first class compartment, a fat, well-dressed gentleman alighted, with a medal ribbon in his buttonhole.

He wore a monocle and white gaiters. His bald patch was concealed beneath a few strands of silvery hair. In his arms he was holding a white Pekinese dog, whose eyes were like two beads of agate floating in olive oil.

For a few moments he walked up and down the platform looking for something. At last, he found it; it was the flower lady. He picked out a few red carnations and paid for them, taking the money from an elegant, supple *port-monnaie* with a silver monogram.

Then, he climbed back into the train carriage and I could see how he placed the lapdog on the little table by the window and fed it the red carnations one after the other, which the animal gulped down with visible gusto…

A terrible shudder awoke me.

It was raining heavily now. The raindrops were pattering beside me and I had to squeeze up against the wall. The sky had turned black and in the distance the town was no longer visible.

I was cold and yet my cheeks were burning. I felt their heat beneath the crust of congealed mud. I wanted to stand up but an electric current flashed through my legs. They were wholly numb and I had to part them, slowly, one after the other. My socks were cold and wet.

I thought about taking shelter in the hut. But the door was locked and, for a window, the hovel had only an opening nailed up with planks. The wind was whipping the rain in all directions and there was nowhere I could protect myself from it.

Night was falling. In a very short time the field would be plunged into darkness. At its very edge, whence I had come, a tavern had lit its lamps.

In an instant I was there; I would have liked to enter, to drink something, to sit in the warmth among people and the reek of alcohol. I rummaged in my pockets and found not a single penny. In front of the tavern the rain was falling heavily through the curtain of smoke and steam that reeked from within.

I had to make up my mind to do something, for example to go home. But how?

In the filthy state I was in that was not possible. But nor did I wish to relinquish my filth.

Into my soul descended an unutterable bitterness, such as a man might experience when he sees that before him there lies absolutely nothing else to do, nothing else to achieve.

I began to run along the streets in the dark, leaping over some puddles and splashing into others up to my knees.

Within me, the despair tumefied for an instant, as though I ought to have screamed and struck my head against the trees. Straightaway, however, this whole sadness bunched up into a tranquil and gentle thought. Now I knew what I had to do: since nothing could go on any longer, it remained only for me to have done with everything. What would I leave behind? A wet, ugly world, in which it was raining slowly…

12

I went into the house by the back door. I stole through the rooms and avoided looking at myself in the mirrors. I was seeking something efficacious and quick that would all at once tip into the dark everything I saw and felt, just as a cart empties of rubble when you pull out the plank from the bottom.

I began to rummage through drawers, in search of a violent poison. As I rummaged, not a single thought came into my head; I had to finish it and as quickly as possible. It was as if I had to complete a task like any other.

I found all kinds of objects that were of no use to me: buttons, twine, coloured thread, playing cards, all strongly smelling of mothballs. So many things that could not cause the death of a man. This is what the world contained at the most tragic moments: buttons, threads, and twine…

At the bottom of a drawer I came upon a box of white tablets. It might be a poison, just as it might be an innocuous medicament. It passed my mind, however, that taken in large quantities it would have to be poisonous.

I placed one tablet on my tongue. In my mouth there spread a slightly salty and bland taste. I crushed it between my teeth and its dust absorbed all my saliva. My mouth turned dry.

There were many tablets in the box, more than thirty. I went to the tap in the yard and slowly, patiently, I made myself swallow them.

For each tablet I took a mouthful of water and it took me a long time to finish the box. The last ones no longer slid down, as if my throat had swollen.

In the yard the darkness was total. I sat on a step and began to wait. In my stomach there started a dreadful burning, but otherwise I felt fine and the pattering of the rain seemed to me ineffably intimate. It seemed to understand my state and to pierce me deeply, to make me well.

The yard became a kind of salon and in it I felt light, ever lighter. All things were making desperate efforts not to drown in obscurity. All of a sudden, I realised that I was sweating terribly. I thrust my hand into my shirt and pulled it out wet. Around me the emptiness was growing vertiginously. When, in the house, I flung myself down on my bed, the sweat bathed me from head to foot.

*

It was a handsome head, extraordinarily handsome.

Around three times larger than a human head, slowly rotating on a bronze axis that transfixed it from crown to throat.

At first all I could descry was the nape. What could it be made of? It had the dull lustre of old faience, with nuances of ivory. The whole surface was imprinted with little blue drawings, a kind of filigree that repeated itself geometrically, like the pattern on linoleum. From afar it seemed like tiny, fine handwriting on ivory paper; unimaginably beautiful.

All of a sudden the head began to move, rotating on its axis, and I was overcome by a profound vertigo. I knew that in a few seconds the face of the cranium would appear – the terrifying, dreadful visage.

It was a visage otherwise well proportioned, with all the usual human contours: sunken eyes, a very prominent chin and a triangle scooped out under each cheek bone, as in the face of a thin man.

The skin, however, was fantastical: made of fine blades of flesh, one next to the other, like the coffee-coloured lamellae under a mushroom cap.

There were so many blades and so tightly packed that if you gazed at the head, closing your eyelids slightly, it did not appear out of the ordinary, and the minuscule lines resembled the crosshatching of an etching.

In summer, sometimes, when I used to see chestnut trees from afar, laden with leaves, their appearance was that of enormous heads stuck on the trunks, with deeply sunken faces, like the lamellae of the head.

When the wind blew through the leaves, the face undulated like the ripples of a cornfield.

The head rustled in the same way, when its pedestal shook.

In order to know that the face was made of wafers it was enough for me only slightly to poke my finger into the flesh. The finger entered without resistance, like into a moist, soft mush. When I pulled it out, the lamellae moved back into place, leaving no visible trace.

In childhood once, I was present at the exhumation and re-interment of a corpse.

It was the corpse of a woman who had died young and had been buried in bridal veils.

The silk bodice had unravelled in long, dirty strips and in places fragments of embroidery were mixed with the earth. But the girl seemed intact and preserved almost all her features. Her colour was livid, so that the head seemed moulded from cardboard soaked in water.

When the coffin was brought up, someone ran his hand across the dead girl's face. Then all the onlookers had a terrible surprise: what we had thought was a well-preserved cheek was nothing but a thick layer of mould, some two fingers deep. The mould had replaced the flesh of the face for the entire depth of the skin, preserving its contours intact. Beneath was bare bone.

And this was what the head was like, the only difference being that instead of mould it was covered with lamellae of flesh. But with my finger, I could poke through them as far as the bone.

The head, although hideous, was a sound refuge against the air.

Wherefore against the air? In the room, the air was forever in motion, colloidal, heavy, runny, trying to congeal into black, ugly stalactites.

It was in this air that the head appeared for the first time and around it there formed a void, like an ever-growing aureole.

I was so pleased and joyous at its emergence that I felt like laughing. But how could I laugh out loud in bed, at night, in the dark?

I began to love the head insatiably. It was the most precious and most intimate thing I possessed. It came from the world of darkness whence reached me only a faint hum, like a continual simmering in my head. What other things were to be found there? I opened my eyes wide and peered vainly into the obscurity. Besides the ivory head nothing else came.

I wondered with a certain fright whether this head would not become in my life the centre of all my preoccupations, replacing everything else, in turn, so that in the end only it and the dark would remain. Life then seemingly took on a precise, authentic meaning. For an instant, it had grown into the air, like a swollen fruit reaching ripeness.

The head was my repose and my beatitude; mine alone. Perhaps if it had belonged to the whole world a dreadful catastrophe would have occurred. A single moment of total happiness would have been capable of petrifying the world for all eternity.

Ever more powerless, the greasy flow of air went on fighting against the "head".

At times, next to it, my father would appear, but vaguely and obliquely, like a mass of bluish vapours. I knew that he would place his hand on my forehead; the hand was cold. I was trying to explain the struggle between the head and the air, while I felt my father unbutton my shirt and slide the thermometer under my armpit, like a slender glass lizard.

Around the head an irritating movement, like the fluttering of a flag, had started up.

Impossible to stop; the banner kept waving.

I remembered that day when at teatime, on the upper floor of Weber's house, Paul had let his hand hang down, over the side of the chair, and Edda, from the bed, raising her shoe a little, had begun jestingly to rub his palm. That gesture had in time taken on an unusual virulence. When I recollected it, the shoe would begin to rub Paul's palm frantically, until a small wound formed, then a hole in the flesh. The shoe did not pause even for an instant in its irritating mechanical movement: it kept scooping out the hole in the palm, and then the entire arm, the entire body…

And this is how the movement of the banner began in my room. It now risked boring a hole in everything, devouring me, perhaps…

I screamed in desperation, wet with sweat.

"How high?" A voice from the shadow.

"Thirty-nine", replied my father, and went out, leaving me prey to the heightening whirlwinds.

13

Convalescence announced its arrival one morning in the form of an extreme fragility of the light. In the room in which I was sleeping, it came through a grooved skylight in the ceiling. The volume of the room queerly decreased in density. The clarity of things weighed lighter and however deeply I breathed, a spacious void remained in my chest, like the disappearance of a significant quantity of myself.

In the warm sheets, crumbs were sliding beneath my thighs. My leg sought the iron of the bedstead and the iron pierced it like a cold blade.

I tried to get out of bed. Everything was as I had suspected: the air was too flimsy to be able to bear my weight. I stepped into it loosely as though I were crossing a steamy, lukewarm river.

I sat down on a chair, below the skylight. Around me the light put the exactitude of things to flight. It was as though it were thoroughly washing them to remove their shine.

The bed, in its corner, lay submerged in darkness. How, in that obscurity, had I managed to make out the wall, during my fever, with its every granule of whitewash?

I began slowly to get dressed; the clothes, too, weighed much lighter than usual. They hung from my body like pieces of blotting paper and smelled of lye from the clothes iron.

Floating through ever-thinner waters, I went out into the street. The sun dizzied me straight away. Huge yellow and greenish glinting blotches partly obscured the houses and passers-by. The street itself seemed thin and fresh, as if it too were emerging from the fever of a serious illness.

The coach horses, grey and unsaddled, were moving abnormally. Now they were walking very slowly, clumsily and unsteadily – now they were bolting, snorting heavily so as not to collapse exhausted in the middle of the asphalt.

The long corridor of houses swayed slightly in the wind. A strong scent of autumn came from afar. "A beautiful autumn day!" I said to myself. "A splendid autumn day!"

I walked very slowly along the length of the dusty houses. In the window of a bookshop I espied a mechanical toy twitching.

It was a small red and blue clown clashing two minuscule brass cymbals. It was shut up there in its room, in the window, among books, balls and pots of ink, and it was clashing its cymbals indifferently, vigorously.

Tears of sadness welled up in my eyes. It was so clean, so cool, and so nice in that corner of the window!

Indeed, an ideal place in this world to stand quietly and bang cymbals, dressed in gaily coloured clothes.

After such a long fever, here was something that was simple and clear. In the shop window, the autumn light fell more intimately, more pleasantly. How good it would have been to take the place of that little, jolly clown! Amid books and balls, surrounded by clean objects nicely laid out on a sheet of blue paper. Bang! Bang! Bang! How good, how good it is in the window! Bang! Bang! Bang! Red, green, blue; balls, books and paints. Bang! Bang! Bang! What a beautiful autumn day! …

Slowly, however, imperceptibly, the clown's movements grew calmer. First of all, the cymbals no longer touched, then, all of a sudden, the clown's arms remained petrified in mid-air.

I realised almost with terror that the clown had stopped playing. Something within me petrified painfully. A beautiful and jolly moment had frozen in the air.

I quickly left the shop window and headed towards a small public garden in the centre of town.

The chestnut trees had shed their yellowed leaves. The old clapboard restaurant was closed and in front of it there sat a disordered host of broken benches.

I sank onto a bench, which was somehow hollowed out in such a way that I found myself almost supine, gazing up at the sky. The sun was radiating a chopped-up, crystalline light through the branches.

For a while I sat there with my gaze lost in the upper air; I was frail, unspeakably frail.

All of a sudden a burly lad sat down next to me, his shirtsleeves rolled up, his neck ruddy and strong, his hands large and dirty. He scratched his head with all ten fingers for a few seconds, then pulled from his trouser pocket a book and began to read.

He held the pages tightly so that the wind would not ruffle them and read muttering loudly; from time to time he ran his hand through his hair, in order to understand the better.

I coughed meaningfully and interrupted him: "What are you reading?" I asked, capsized on the bench, my eyes on the branches of the trees.

The lad placed the book in my hand as though I were a blind man. It was a long tale in verse about haidouks, a greasy book, full of fat stains and filth; it was obvious that it had passed through many hands. While I was looking at it, he stood up and remained there in front of me, strong, self-confident, his sleeves rolled up, his neck bare.

Something as pleasant and as calm as banging cymbals in a shop window.

"And... doesn't your head ache when you read?" I asked him, giving back the book.

He seemed not to understand.

"Why should it ache? It doesn't ache at all", he said and sat down on the bench once more to carry on reading.

There was thus a category of things in the world of which I was destined never to be part, impassive and mechanical clowns, burly lads whose heads never ached. Around me, among the trees, in the light of the sun, a lively, broad current flowed, full of life and purity. I was destined forever to remain at its edge, sullied by darkness and fainting fits.

I stretched my legs out on the bench, and leaning my back against a tree I found a very comfortable position. In the end, what was stopping me, too, from being strong and impassive? From feeling a vigorous and fresh sap circulating within me, the same as it circulates through the tree's thousands of branches and leaves, from standing straight and meaninglessly in the sun, erect, sober, with an assured and well-defined life, a life sprung inside me like a trap...

For this perhaps I would first have to breathe more deeply and more slowly: I breathed poorly, my chest was always too full or too empty. A thin fluid of perfection, but one I felt swelling every moment, began to flow through my veins. The noise of the street reminded me of the distant town, but now the town was revolving very slowly around me, like a gramophone record. I had become something like the axis of the globe, for example. What was of the essence was not to lose my balance.

Once, at the circus, one morning, while the artistes were rehearsing, I witnessed a scene that now comes back to my mind... An amateur from the audience, a mere spectator without any training, climbed, without so much as blinking, with much courage, up a pyramid of chairs and tables which a circus acrobat had ascended a little while before. We all admired the precision with which he scaled the dangerous structure, and the frenzy of having managed to conquer the first obstacles intoxicated the amateur with a kind of reckless knowledge of equilibrium, which caused him to place his hand exactly in the right spot, to stretch out his foot with precision and find in it the minimum weight with which to tackle a new level in height. Dazed and happy at the assurance of his movements, in a few seconds he reached the peak. Here, however, something wholly peculiar took place in him: in an instant he realised the fragility of the balancing point he had reached, as well as his extraordinary daring. His teeth chattering, in a faint voice he asked for a ladder and repeatedly advised those below to hold onto it firmly and not to move. The courageous amateur descended with infinite caution, step by step, sweating from head to foot, amazed and annoyed at the idea he had had of climbing.

My position now in the garden was at the peak of a precarious pyramid. I could well feel a new and vigorous sap circulating within me, but I had to force myself not to fall from the heights of my admirable certitude.

It crossed my mind that this was how I ought to see Edda: calmly, self-confidently, full of light. I had not gone there for a long time. I wished at least once to present myself whole and imperturbable in front of someone.

As silent and superb as a tree. That was it – like a tree. I filled my chest with air and stretching my back, I bade a warm, comradely farewell to the branches above me. There was something harsh and simple in a tree, which was wonderfully akin to my new powers. I stroked the trunk as though I were patting the shoulder of a friend. "Comrade tree!" The more carefully I looked at the infinitely dispersed crown of the branches, the better I felt within me... the flesh dividing and the living air from without beginning to circulate through its cavities. The blood was rising in me majestically and full of sap, frothing with the ebullition of the simple life.

I rose to my feet. For a moment my knees bent uncertainly, as if they wanted to compare, by means of a single hesitation, all my strength and my weakness. With long strides I headed towards Edda's house.

The heavy wooden door that opened onto the balcony was closed. Its inertness dazed me slightly. My every last thought flew away.

I placed my hand on the door handle and pressed. "Courage", I told myself, but I paused to rectify it. "Courage? Only timid people need the courage to do something; normal people, strong people have neither courage nor cowardice, they quite simply open doors, like this…"

The cool darkness of the first room overwhelmed me, with an atmosphere that was calm and joyful, as if it had been expecting me for a long time.

This time, the bead curtain made a bizarre clink as it closed behind me, which made it seem that I was alone in a deserted house at the edge of the world. Was this the sensation of extreme equilibrium at the peak of the pyramid of chairs?

I knocked loudly on Edda's door.

Affrighted, she bid me enter. Why was I treading so softly?

"Was I treading softly?" It nonetheless seemed to me that the presence of a person such as myself, or, more accurately speaking, of a tree, should be felt from afar.

In the room, however, no surprise, no excitement, not even the slightest emotion, was stirred.

For a few seconds my thoughts had preceded me in an ideal way, with a great perfection and sobriety of gesture. I saw myself advancing very confidently, and, with a nonchalant movement, seating myself at Edda's feet on the bed where she lay stretched. My real person had, however, been left in the wake of those beautiful plans, like a worthless, broken trailer.

Edda invited me to sit and arranged a chair for me at a great distance from her.

Between us the pendulum clock was beating out an irritating and very sonorous tick-tock. A curious thing: the tick-tock swelled and receded like the ebb and flow of the sea, moving in a wave towards Edda until I could barely hear it and then returning towards me, swollen, so loud that it burst my eardrums.

"Edda", I began to say, interrupting the silence, "allow me to tell you something very simple…"

Edda made no reply.

"Edda, do you know what I am?"

"What are you?"

"A tree, Edda, a tree…"

This entire short conversation took place, of course, strictly inside me and not a single word was really uttered.

Edda nestled on the bed, curling her knees under her and covering them with the peignoir. Then she placed her hands at the back of her head and gazed at me closely. I would joyfully have given anything to find another point in the room from which to look at her.

All of a sudden I saw a large bouquet of flowers on a shelf: in a vase. It was this that saved me.

How had I not seen them up until then? I had been looking in that direction since I entered the room. In order to verify their having appeared, I looked in another direction and came back to them. There they were in their place, immobile, large, red... How then had I not seen them? I began to doubt my tree-like confidence. Here was an object that had appeared in the room where it had not been a moment before. Was my eyesight always clear? Perhaps in my body there had remained traces of impotence and darkness that were circulating through my new luminosity like clouds across a brilliant sky, occluding my sight when they passed through the humour of my eyes, just as clouds against the sky suddenly cover the sun and plunge a part of the landscape into darkness.

"How beautiful those flowers are", I said to Edda.

"What flowers?"

"Those ones, on the shelf..."

"What flowers?"

"Those beautiful red dahlias..."

"What dahlias?"

"What do you mean... 'What dahlias'?"

I stood up and rushed to the shelf. Tossed onto a heap of books there lay a red scarf. In the instant when I stretched out my hand and convinced myself that it really was a scarf, something hesitated in me, from afar, like an oscillation in the courage of an amateur balancing artist, at the peak of a pyramid, midway between acrobatics and dilettantism. I, too, had, of course, reached my extreme limit of altitude.

The whole problem now was to turn around and to sit back down on the chair. And thereafter what should I do, what should I say?

For a few moments I was so stupefied by this problem that it was impossible for me to make the slightest movement. Like the high speeds of a machine flywheel which make it seem motionless, my profoundly desperate hesitation lent me the rigidity of a statue. The tick-tock of the clock was throbbing loudly, riveting me with tiny sonic nails. I tore myself from my immobility with the greatest difficulty.

Edda was in the same position on the bed, looking at me in exactly the same calm astonishment; one might have said that a malefic, highly perfidious power rendered things in their most usual appearance in order to place me in the greatest quandary. This was what was fighting against me, this was what was implacably against me: the usual appearance of things.

In a world so exact, any initiative became superfluous, if not impossible. What made the blood rush to my head was that Edda could not be otherwise, but rather nothing more than a woman with well-brushed hair, with violet-blue eyes, with a smile at the corner of her lips. What could I do against such a harsh exactitude? How could I make her understand, for example, that I was a tree? What was to be conveyed, through the air, in immaterial and formless words, was a superb and enormous crown of branches and leaves such as I felt within me. How could I do that?

I approached the bed and leaned upon the wooden rail. My hands radiated a kind of certainty, as though the entire node of my disquiet had suddenly descended into them.

Well, what now? Between Edda and me stood the same pellucid, vertiginous air, impalpable and apparently insubstantial, in which nonetheless slumbered all my powers, powers unable to achieve anything. That wretched volume had room for hesitations weighing dozens of pounds, silences hours long, disquietude, and vertigo made flesh and blood, but it had no external aspect that might reveal the black colouring and the nebulous matter it contained. In the world, distances were not simply those we saw with our infirm and permeable eyes, but rather they were invisible, thronged with monsters and timidities – with fantastical plans and unsuspected gestures, which, if for an instant they had coagulated into the matter of which they tended to be composed, would have transformed the outward appearance of the world into a terrifying cataclysm, into an extraordinary chaos, full of cruel misfortunes and ecstatic beatitudes.

At that moment, looking at Edda, perhaps the materialisation of my thoughts would indeed have resulted in that simple gesture that was droning in my head: to lift the paperweight from the table (I could see it from the corner of my eye; it was a noble mediaeval helmet, weighing down the paper) and cast it at Edda. As an immediate consequence, a stupendous spout of blood would have spurted from her chest, like the jet of water from a tap. It would have gradually filled the room, until I felt the warm, sticky liquid lapping first against my feet, then my knees, and then – like in those sensational American films where a character is doomed to stand in a hermetically sealed room in which the water is rising ever higher – it would have reached my mouth, drowning me in the salty, pleasant taste of blood…

My lips started moving involuntarily and I swallowed.

"Are you hungry?" asked Edda.

"Well, no, no… I'm not hungry, I was thinking of something… absurd… completely absurd".

"Please tell me. Since you came you haven't spoken a single word and I haven't asked you anything… now I'm waiting, as you can see".

"Look, Edda", I began, "ultimately it's something very simple, really quite simple… forgive me for telling you, but I…"

I wanted to add, "I am a tree", but the phrase no longer had any value now that I thirsted to drink blood. It lay colourless and withered at the bottom of my soul and I was amazed that it could ever have possessed any importance.

I began over again.

"Look, Edda, this is the thing, I'm ill, I was feeling weak and wretched. Your presence always makes me feel better, it's enough for me to see you… are you annoyed about this?"

"Not at all…" she replied and began to laugh.

I now really felt like doing something absurd, bloody, violent. I quickly picked up my hat. "I'm leaving". In an instant I was at the bottom of the stairs.

Now something was for sure: the world had its own habitual outward appearance, into the midst of which I had fallen by mistake, I would never be able to become a tree, or to kill someone, and nor would the blood ever spurt in torrents. All things, all people, were enclosed in their sad, petty obligation to be precise, nothing more than precise. In vain might I have believed that there were dahlias in a vase, when it was a scarf. The world did not have the power to change in the slightest; it was so ignobly enclosed in its precision that it could not allow itself to mistake a scarf for flowers…

For the first time I felt my head tightly clenched in the bone of my cranium, terrifyingly and painfully imprisoned…

14

That autumn, Edda fell ill and died. In all the anterior days, all my aimless walks, all my efforts and all my tortured questions accumulated into the pain and disquietude of a single week, just as in those liquids where the mixture of a number of substances all of a sudden condenses into a powerful poison.

Over the upper floor yet another species of silence settled. Paul had managed to find, in some cupboard or other, an old raincoat and a threadbare necktie, knotted around his throat like twine. He had a bluish colour, like a fine veil left by sleepless nights upon his cheek.

"She suffered all night", he told me. "Yesterday, I asked the doctor yet again what he thought and he told me everything, the whole truth. It's as if something had exploded in her kidneys, the doctor confessed to me. It's extremely rare for an illness like this to appear so virulently, and so suddenly. Usually, it takes hold slowly, with the symptoms that herald it, long before it becomes serious. There has been an explosion in her kidneys; a real explosion".

Paul was talking quickly but with long pauses, as though between the words he wished to allow time for an acute pain to come to the boil in him, to reach perfection.

The office below was plunged into darkness, like in a cave; old man Weber, with his head in a ledger, was giving the illusion of being busy…

Every morning the doctor came with silent footfalls and as he passed through the rooms the three Webers followed him.

I brought up the rear, talking with Ozy. It had been a long time since I had played our imaginary game and now would have been a wonderful occasion.

How good it would have been for us to talk about Edda's illness as if nothing had happened!

Climbing the stairs I thought about the extraordinary possibility of a game conducted by Ozy, in which the doctor and Paul Weber and the old man would take part. Let the hunchback direct, just this once, an imagined and non-existent play. When I reached the upper floor, I felt like shouting: "That's enough already, it's all over, it was well acted, Paul really did have an impressive mask, it was obvious old man Weber was suffering, but now it's enough, it's finished, please tell them, Ozy, not to bother with the rest…"

But everything was too well arranged for it to stop at the top of the stairs…

While the doctor was with Edda, I would remain in the next room with old man Weber and Ozy.

It was perhaps the first time in his life when old man Weber had tried to master a strong emotion. With head bowed, from an armchair he would gaze outside impersonally and vaguely, as if he neither knew nor expected anything. At last, like those great actors who tend to perfect their role by means of some unusual detail, he would rise from the armchair and go to look more closely at a painting on the wall. Like the great actor, however, who raising his voice too loudly for a tragic outburst transforms it into a bellow worthy of laughter from the stalls, old man Weber, in trying to play the role with too much calm, would botch the effect: while he stood looking at the painting he would be drumming his fingers irritably on a chair behind him…

Paul took me by the hand:

"Edda wishes to see you, come with me, quietly".

In the bed with the white sheets Edda was lying with her face toward the window. Her hair was spread over the pillows, blonder and finer than ever before: illnesses possess such subtleties. In the room there reigned a kind of white decomposition of things, with horribly abundant light; Edda's face vanished into it, insubstantially.

All of a sudden she turned her head.

But it was true… I mean, in that moment, something occurred in me that was so indistinct, so lucid, and so surprising that it might have constituted a truth from beyond… Edda's head wholly resembled that ivory head from my nights of fever. This evidence was so vertiginous that it even occurred to me that I had invented in that instant the exact form of the old faience head, with the compositional speed of those dreams that create an entire episode in the moment when we hear the noise of a shot.

I was now certain that something violent and evil would soon happen to Edda. Perhaps I later imagined this thing too; as regards Edda, I cannot discern anything of what I myself might be and what she was.

She sought to gaze into my eyes but closed her eyelids, exhausted. Her swept-back hair highlighted the yellow forehead, like a block of wax. I was once more hermetically closed within Edda's presence, within what she represented now and in my nights of delirium. In none of my walks, in none of my encounters had I truly thought of anyone else except myself. It was impossible for me to conceive of another's inner pain, or quite simply another's existence. The persons I saw around me were as decorative, as ephemeral and as material as any other object, such as houses or trees. Only in front of Edda, for the first time, did I feel that my questions might be unleashed and, resonating in other depths and in another existence, come back to me in enigmatic and troubling echoes.

Who was Edda? What was Edda? For the first time I saw myself on the outside, because in Edda's presence it was the question of the meaning of my life. It shook me more deeply and more authentically at the moment of her death; her death was my death and in everything I have done since then, in everything I have experienced, the immobility of my future death projects itself, cold and obscure, the same as I saw it in Edda.

*

At dawn that day I awoke heavy and stony, embarrassed by the presence of someone at my bedside.

It was my father, who had been waiting in silence for me to awake. When I opened my eyes, he took a few paces across the room, and fetched me a white basin and a cup of water to wash my hands.

With a painful convulsion that gripped my heart I understood what this meant.

"Wash your hands", my father told me. "Edda has died".

It was drizzling outside and the rain did not stop for three days.

On the day of the funeral the mud was more aggressive and filthier than ever. The wind blew volleys of water onto roofs and windows. The whole night a window had remained illumined on the upper floor of the Weber house, in the room where the candles were burning.

In the office of old man Weber, everything had been turned upside down and moved to one side to allow the coffin to pass; the mud entered the rooms; triumphant and insinuating, like a hydra with countless protoplasmic protuberances, I saw very well how it spread along the walls, crawling up the people, climbing the stairs and attempting to scale the coffin.

Downstairs, in the office, the wooden floorboards were visible. The carpet that had hidden them had been removed. Long wrinkles of dirt appeared, like the black lines that had grown deeper in Samuel Weber's face.

Around his *gomme élastique* boots the mud climbed slowly but tenaciously, undoubtedly penetrating through the skin as far as the heart, filthy, heavy, sticky. There was mud and nothing else. There was the floor and nothing else. There were the candles and nothing else. "My funeral will be a succession of objects", Edda had once told me.

Something in me was struggling somewhere far away, as if it wished to prove to me the existence of a truth higher than the mud, something that would be other than mud. In vain... My identity had long since become veritable and now, in a most ordinary way, all it did was to verify itself: in the world nothing existed besides the mud. What I took to be pain was in me nothing more than its faint swarming, a protoplasmic protuberance moulded from words and reasons.

The droplets streamed into Paul as if into a bottomless vessel. His clothes streamed over him; his arms streamed, dangling heavily, causing his back to bow. The tears trickled down his dirty face, in long streaks, like water down a windowpane.

Slowly, balanced on the shoulders of the pallbearers, the coffin passed Samuel Weber's ship, the old ledgers and the dozens of pots of ink and the medicaments brought to light while the office was being cleared out. The funeral was a mere succession of objects.

A number of other details also occurred, beyond life: in the cemetery, when they removed the corpse from the coffin, wrapped in white sheets, the sheets bore the trace of a large bloodstain.

It was the final and most insignificant detail before the subsoil of the cemetery, warm, mouldering, and full of bodies as soft as gelatine, yellow... purulent...

15

Over and over again, I recollect these things, trying in vain to bind them together into something that I might call my own self. As I recollect them, old man Weber's office all of a sudden becomes the very room in which I am breathing the mould and odour of old ledgers, only to vanish forthwith, giving way to a real room that raises the same painful question of the way in which people spend their lives. Lives in which they rely, for example, on rooms, or else feel as if they were like an alien body in those rooms, ramifying like a fern, as insubstantial as smoke. Then, all of a sudden, there is a distinct odour, like the profoundly enigmatic odour of mould. Events and people spread open and shut within me like fans. My hand tries to set down on paper this strange and incomprehensible simplicity. And it is then for an instant – like a condemned man who in a flash comprehends that the death awaiting him is different to that of all the men around him, and who would like his agony to be different to all the other agonies in the world, an agony that might release him – that from all these things there seems suddenly to emerge, warm and intimate, a new and authentic deed that might sum me up as clearly as a name and resound in me like a unique, hithero unheard note. A note in which will resound the meaning of my life…

Why else, if not for the sake of these things, does there persist in me this fluid, so intimate and nevertheless so hostile, so close and nevertheless so refractory to capture, which of itself transforms into the image of Edda or into the bowed shoulders of Paul Weber or into the excessively precise detail of a dripping tap in the corridor of a hotel?

Why does the memory of Edda's final days come back to me so clearly now? Why, albeit posing the question in a different sense (and questions too can grow chaotically into thousands and thousands of different senses, like in that game from childhood when I used to fold a piece of paper with an ink blot and press hard so that the ink would spread, and when I opened the paper it would reveal the most fantastical and unsuspected contortions of a bizarre drawing), is it that this memory and no other comes back to me?

Each memory, incomprehensible and exact, ought to make me aware yet again of its uniqueness. It is like the violent pain of a sick man, which overshadows his momentary little pangs of discomfort, such as an awkwardly positioned pillow or the bitterness of a medicament. It is like a pain that envelops and overwhelms all my other puzzlements and disquietudes. And what I ought to be aware of is that, however lowly and incomprehensible it might appear, each memory is nevertheless unique, in the most impoverished meaning of the word, and has occurred in my life in a single, precise, linear way, without any possibility of modification or the slightest deviation from its own precision.

"Your life was thus and not otherwise", memory says, and in this sentence resides the immense nostalgia of this world, a nostalgia enclosed in its lights and hermetic colours, from which not one single life is allowed to extract anything other than the appearance of a precise banality.

In it resides the melancholy of being unique and limited, in a unique and ignobly arid world.

Sometimes, at night, I awake from a terrible nightmare. It is my most simple and terrifying dream.

I dream that I am sleeping deeply, in the bed where I lay down the evening before. It is the same setting and approximately the same time of night. If, for example, the nightmare begins at midnight, it places me in precisely the same kind of darkness and silence that reigns at that hour. In the dream I see and feel the position in which I find myself. I know in which bed and in which room it is that I am sleeping. My dream moulds itself like a fine skin over my actual posture and over my sleep in that moment. In this regard, it might be said that I am awake: I am awake, but I am sleeping and dreaming of my being awake. I am also dreaming my sleep in that moment.

And all of a sudden I feel how sleep grows deeper, heavier, and seeks to draw me down after it.

I want to wake up and sleep weighs heavily on my eyelids and my hands. I dream that I am struggling, waving my hands, but sleep is stronger than me and after I have floundered for an instant, it overwhelms me all the more heavily and more tenaciously. Then I start to scream, I want to resist sleep, I want somebody to wake me, I violently slap myself to wake myself up, I am afraid that sleep will submerge me too deeply, whence I shall never be able to come back, I beg somebody to help me, to shake me…

In the end, my final scream, the loudest, wakes me. All of a sudden I find myself in my real room, which is identical to the room in the dream, and in the same position in which I dreamt myself, at the same hour when I must have been floundering in the nightmare.

What I now see around me differs very little from what I saw only a second before, but somehow it has an air of authenticity, which floats in things, in me, like a sudden cooling of the winter air, which all of a sudden magnifies all sonorities...

In what does my sense of reality consist?

Around me the life I will live until the next dream has returned. Memories and present pains weigh heavily in me and I want to resist them, not to fall into their sleep, whence I shall perhaps never return...

Now I am struggling in reality, I scream, I beg to be woken, to be woken to a different life, to my real life. It is certain that it is broad daylight, that I know where I am and that I am alive, but in all these things something is missing, the same as in my terrifying nightmare.

I struggle, scream, writhe. Who will wake me?

Around me, a precise reality is pulling me ever lower, trying to submerge me.

Who will wake me?

It has always been like this, always, always.

The Author

What makes Max Blecher akin to Kafka, Bruno Schulz or Robert Walser is above all the faculty of inhabiting misfortune, of accepting it as a condition of ongoing life. Before the disease manifests itself, he observes a systematic aggression against him on the part of the universe. Things emerge from their neutrality and besiege him, seeking to fascinate or terrorise him.

Ovid Crohmălniceanu (*prominent communist era and post-war critic*)

Max Blecher (1909 – 1938), poet and prose writer, offers a harrowing account of the "bizarre adventure of being a man" that draws upon his experience, in 1928, of being diagnosed with tuberculosis of the spine (Pott's disease). He was treated in various sanatoria in France, Switzerland and Romania, but to no avail. Engagement with existentialist philosophy led to an interest in Surrealism. Without joining any particular grouping he corresponded with, among others, Geo Bogza, Mihail Sebastian, André Breton, André Gide, Martin Heidegger and Ilarie Voronca, and sporadically collaborated with the Paris-based magazines *Le Surréalisme au service de la révolution* and *Les Feuillets inutiles.*

Other writings include *Scarred Hearts* (1937), *The Illumined Burrow* (published posthumously in part 1947, in full 1971), *Transparent Body* (1934).

Couple (detail)
Oil on canvas 2007

The Translator

Alistair Ian Blyth was born in Sunderland in 1970 and educated at Bede School, Cambridge University (BA), and Durham University (MA). From Romanian he has translated a number of works, including *An Intellectual History of Cannibalism* by Cătălin Avramescu (Princeton University Press), the novel *Little Fingers* by Filip Florian (Houghton-Mifflin Harcourt), the novel *Our Circus Presents...* by Lucian Dan Teodorovici (Dalkey Archive Press), *Aunt Varvara's Clients: Clandestine Histories* by Stelian Tănase (Spuyten Duyvil), and two books by Constantin Noica; *Six Maladies of the Contemporay Spirit* (University of Plymouth Press) and *The Becoming within Being* (Marquette UP). He lives in Bucharest.

Point of Balance (detail)
Oil on canvas, 2008

20 Romanian Writers

Publications November 2009

Six Maladies of the Contemporary Spirit
Constantin Noica

Posthumously awarded the Herder Prize, 1988
ISBN 978-1-84102-203-1 Hardback

In this unique work, Noica analyses history, culture and the individual in what he describes as the fundamental precariousness of being. 'Maladies' of the spirit are no longer debilitating, but creative for our European interest in change, unity, and diversity.

Lines Poems Poetry
Mircea Ivănescu

Botoşani Mihai Eminescu National Poetry Prize, 1999
ISBN 978-1-84102-217-8 Hardback

Ivănescu's poetry represents the achievement of a little known master. Centring on a wide cast of characters, including his alter ego 'mopete', Ivănescu's idiosyncratic, lyrical sensibility offers allusive, comic and elegiac meditations on our common lot.

The Cinematography Caravan
Ioan Groşan

Romanian Writers' Union, Prize for Prose, 1992
ISBN 978-1-84102-205-5 Hardback

A black comedy set in 1960s Romania: a Stalinist propaganda film truck rumbles into a forgotten Transylvanian village. The occupants of the village believe in the traditional values of church and God and are in no mood to participate, placing obstacles in the way of the Cinematography Caravan crew. The resultant humour is deliberately provincial as the villagers find their own unique ways of dealing with them while they're in town.

November 2010

Ieud with No Exit
Ioan Es Pop

Romanian Order of Cultural Merit, 2004
ISBN 978-1-84102-209-3 Hardback

Originally a teacher in Ieud, Ioan Es Pop's poetry expresses his response to his existence in a Romania under communist control, forbidden to write but able to work as a builder on Ceauşescu's palace and living alone in a bachelor block. Pop's poetry is an autobiographical account of such a time, a life without any magical exit. In the village of Ieud some confused his poetry with reality suggesting that if he did return then there would be no exit from Ieud.

Dazzler
Mircea Cărtărescu

Grand Officer of the Cultural Merit Order, awarded by the Romanian Presidency, 2006
ISBN 978-1-84102-206-2 Hardback

The first book in the Dazzler Trilogy describes a communist Bucharest awash with thrills and nightmares. Dazzler opens with a sixties bedroom view obscured by towering prefab blocks - a Romania in rupture. His writing is influenced by childhood memories; hearing the screams of political prisoners being interrogated and only now revisiting these places as they are gradually torn down. The essence of Cărtărescu is to capture the socialist capital leading up to the moment of its downfall.
This title within the 20 Romanian Writers series is subject to change with another Mircea Cărtărescu publication.

French Themes
Nicolae Manolescu

Romanian Ambassador to UNESCO, 2006
Romanian Academy Member, 2007
ISBN 978-1-84102-208-6 Hardback

Inspired by the combination of political intrigue and love contained within the belles lettres of the great French novelists, Manolescu uses this recipe to tell the story of a great love. Cristina Chevereşan considers French Themes as "love declared or merely suggested, patient and durable, arousing the aromas of French perfumes but also a reading in culture and civilization".

Aunt Varvara's Client
Stelian Tănase

Awarded a Fulbright Scholarship, 1997
ISBN 978-1-84102-221-5 Hardback

Stelian Tănase explores Romania's communist 'roots of disaster' from early illegal membership of the communist underground to their eventual rise to power and the struggle for supremacy. Tănase sketches a pattern of warring factions through an incredible swarm of characters who abruptly fall completely silent after the final victory of Gheorghiu-Dej and the formation of the communist police state and its hierarchy. A Romania then on course for human disaster.

November 2011

Who Won the World War of Religions?
Daniel Bănulescu

City of Munster European Poetry Prize, 2005
ISBN 978-1-84102-212-3 Hardback

Contemporary madness in its entirety is summarised in Daniel Bănulescu's play, set in an asylum populated with twelve dangerous madmen who are divided as believers of the four major religions. This is theatre in a world governed by insanity; as Dan Stanca remarks, the play could be set anywhere - in Piteşti, in the Siberian Gulag, in a Nazi concentration camp, Maoist or Khmer Rouge extermination camp, and, even, in one of the CIA's secret prisons? This is the principal merit and black humour of the play.

Wasted Morning
Gabriela Adamesteanu

Romanian Writers' Union Prize for the Novel, 1983
ISBN 978-1-84102-211-6 Hardback

Wasted Morning is a truly modern novel, beginning and ending in the present yet resurrecting a Romania of the past. The story centres on Madam Vica Delcă who visits Ivona Scarlat. During this visit Ivona receives news of her husband's sudden death, triggering memories of the past which are then re-lived. Adamesteanu creates a world of old upper bourgeois Romania at the brink of World War One.

This title within the 20 Romanian Writers series is subject to change with another Gabriela Adamesteanu publication.

Small Changes in Attitude
Răzvan Petrescu

Grand Prize at the 1st Edition of the Camil Petrescu National
Dramaturgic Competition; Romanian Writers' Union Prize for
Theatre, 1995
ISBN 978-1-84102-214-7 Hardback

Răzvan Petrescu is cited by Adriana Bittel as one of Romania's finest short prose writers. This anthology of short fiction paints each story as a photographic reality and journeys from realistic black humor to the ironic and fantastic. This collection includes his 1989 debut, 'Summer Garden', 'Eclipse', a modern take on the biblical story of Cain and Abel, and 'Friday Afternoon' wherein an epidemic kills everyone in an apartment block. The title truly summarizes this anthology; Petrescu suggests small changes in attitude.

Anthology of Poems
Ion Mureşan

Romanian Writers' Union Prize for Poetry, 1993
ISBN 978-1-84102-213-0 Hardback

There is both an enigmatic and an original character to the poetic language of Ion Mureşan who concerns himself with the political nature of Romanian poetry in this anthology. Mureşan's poetry draws upon Transylvanian legends to address the communist manipulation and monopoly of truth by regaining individual thought through his poetry, which reflects upon what it is to be Romanian.

November 2012

Simion the Liftite
Petru Cimpoeşu

Romanian Writers' Union Prize of Cuvîntul, 2001
ISBN 978-1-84102-215-4 Hardback

This novel captures hope and despair in post-revolution Romania. Christ descends for three days at the height of the revolution in December 1989 and stands in the presidential election, offering himself as saviour and sacrifice once again. Mircea Iorgulescu says of Petru Cimpoeşu that there is a permanent ambiguity in this narrative, which never descends into caricature, but rather is viewed with understanding and even, quite often, warmth. The lack of aggression comes from aesthetic style. The serenity of tone here has its origin in the pure pleasure of constructing a story.

Silent Escape and Impossible Escape
Lena Constante

Romanian Academy, Lucain Blaga Prize, 1993
ISBN 978-1-84102-216-1 Hardback

Lena Constante is one of the few women political prisoners to have written about her years of imprisonment. She describes in detail her physical and psychological humiliation and suffering in the solitary confinement common in communist Romania. The whole premise of this novel rests on Constante's ability to survive, to escape into her mind and on solidarity with other female inmates. A work of human survival against the odds.

The Iceberg of Modern Poetry
Gheorghe Crăciun

ASPRO Prize for the Year's Best Book of Criticism 1997, 2002
ISBN 978-1-84102-204-8 Hardback

Gheorghe Crăciun redefines modernist poetry through the analysis of Wordsworth and Coleridge, Baudelaire and Whitman. Through this Crăciun proposes a new direction for modern poetry, one that is in permanent tension. This eventually leads Crăciun to consider a third direction, one that revisits old traditions that are still reflected and reinflected in modern poetry. The Iceberg of Modern Poetry is a 500 page authoritative contribution to international debate on this subject.

Picturesque and Melancholy
Andrei Pleşu

Ordre national de la Légion d'Honneur, to the rank of Commandeur, and then Grand Officier, 1999
ISBN 978-1-84102-218-5 Hardback

Pleşu questions European culture through the aesthetic of melancholy and literary picturesque myths of Western culture. A controversial text at the time it was written, he approaches the topic from a philosophical stance with an exuberant writing style and an undertow of the subversive. He fell out of favour with the communist regime and was banned from publishing which resulted in his exile to Tescani a community in Bacau, Moldova, Romania.

November 2013

Diary of Happiness
Nicolae Steinhardt

ISBN 978-1-84102-210-9 Hardback

Romania was not the place for a Jewish intellectual at a time when the regime was re-Stalinising. Steinhardt could have escaped prison if he became a witness for the prosecution in a communist show trial. He refused and was imprisoned in 1959 for 'high treason' and 'machinating against the socialist order'. These pages are an introspective diary of Steinhardt's prison years, as Romanian literary critic Mircea Martin explains, Diary of Happiness is not only a revelation of faith, but is also a revelation of freedom and of inner freedom.

Little Fingers
Filip Florian

România Literară and Anonimul Foundation Prize for Debut Novel, 2004
ISBN 978-1-84102-219-2 Hardback

Florin takes the reader to a small Romanian mountain village near the ruins of an old Roman fort where a mass grave has been discovered; are these remains medieval or modern? A human atrocity, but is it best to ignore, or confront, the past, any past? Whether ancient, or from the recent past, the grave brings back memories of all that is tragic in the former Ceauşescu's communist Romania. Many characters propel the story forward: the arrival of Argentinean forensic investigators, the priest Onufrie, and, of course, the mystery of missing finger bones, which disappear from the pit each night.
This title within the 20 Romanian Writers series is subject to change with another Filip Florian publication.

The Children's Crusade
Florina Ilis

România Literară and Anonimul Foundation Prize for Book of the
Year, 2005
ISBN 978-1-84102-220-8 Hardback

A train is hijacked by children, who organise resistance against the
authorities sent from Bucharest. In their attempts to negotiate, the
authorities prove hypocritical, lacking any understanding of the
children's demands. The novel presents a clash of ideologies relating to
what it is to be Romanian and to the realities of life under Ceauşescu's
communist rule. Ilis weaves two differing viewpoints together, reversing
perspectives and constructing a world adrift.

Cioran Naïve and Sentimental
Ion Vartic

Romanian Writers' Union Prize, Cluj branch award, essay, 2004
ISBN 978-1-84102-222-2 Hardback

A biography of Emil Cioran, a philosopher and freethinker, born
in Transylvania, who had an inferiority complex and was ashamed of
his birthplace. Cioran was attracted to Western culture, because his
perception was that Eastern European countries have always been
dominated by Western European history. Vartic suggests that Cioran
represents one extreme and that Romanians are proud of their cultural
heritage, taking the virtues of home and making it theirs.

Point of Balance (detail)
Oil on canvas, 2008

Point of Balance (detail)
Oil on canvas, 2008

Touching (detail)
Monotype, 2007